About the Author

Peter is best known as a pianist and vocalist of many years standing, famous for his rock n roll and boogie woogie performances and for touring the UK and Europe in a host of top theatre shows. He has written several non-fiction books and a number of plays. *Meet Tommy Atkins* is his first novel and is based on his play of the same name.

Peter lives in Gloucestershire in the UK.

For more information on him please visit his website: www.petegill.org.uk

Meet Tommy Atkins

Peter Gill

Meet Tommy Atkins

Olympia Publishers
London

www.olympiapublishers.com
OLYMPIA PAPERBACK EDITION

ISBN: 978-1-80074-078-5

First Published in 2021

Olympia Publishers
Tallis House
2 Tallis Street
London
EC4Y 0AB

Printed in Great Britain

Dedication

To all the Tommies who did return and helped to create the country in which we live with all its freedoms, privileges and welfare — *Lest We Forget.*

PART 1
MONS
November 11, 1918

A stranger entering the battered and bruised town would be less overcome by the devastation than by the stench. The evil, acrid odour of war. Not simply the smell of decay and the dead, but also that of the living. Bodies lying silently in their shallow graves, or unfound amongst the debris of battle, gave in to nature, dissolving slowly into the earth that bore them and reminding all, in their final reek, that they had once walked, laughed, sang, talked, made love. The bodies had had dreams and beliefs. Some of them had been the truest of people, others had been the lowest. Some were smart, others could barely string a sentence together. Some had been born with fortunes in their hands, others had made their own wealth, some had started with nothing and ended with nothing. Now they were all as one. A stench.

The air bore their last message and diffused it with a thousand other, equally as potent odours. Piss and shit from men and horses, clung to the atmosphere as if it were painted on the walls of the once proud homes. Woodbines, smoked in their millions, contested to push their sickly-sweet face to the top of the stink pile. Cordite, the signaller of death and torment, filled any void that dared to be. It was a solid wall of stench that no stranger would fail to notice.

Tommy, however, was far from being a stranger.

As he picked his way cautiously, tired and exhausted through the rubble he remained alert, aware that fate and his wits had brought him to this point in his life and only they would lead him further. As he trudged, Tommy smelled nothing that was unfamiliar. Though its tendrils grabbed at him, clawed at his senses and begged him for attention, he failed to notice the stench.

For almost four years he had lived with the perfume of war. He had been blanketed by it, seen where it came from, witnessed it grow and manifest into a spectre and felt the terror that it brought. The stench was a taunting, seducing, gloating whisper reminding him that going home was an optimistic dream — an eternity in Belgian soil was the more likely future that awaited him.

Tommy had long since stopped listening. He had clipped his senses, trained them to ignore the irrelevant and concentrate only on that which would actually threaten his survival. So, as he walked with the stench prodding and tickling at him, it went ignored, unnoticed and unobserved, Tommy remained unmoved by its presence.

It was instead the silence that gripped his attention and filled his thoughts.

A stranger would have said that the air was filled with noise. That there wasn't a silent molecule of atmosphere. All was a chaotic smorgasbord of raised voices. Some were shouting boisterously, others relentlessly cheering. There was laughter and singing and somewhere underneath it all, like a thin and well-worn mattress there was weeping. Amongst the voices, a stranger would have been aware of the constant sound of movement as men, beasts and motors journeyed through the area. To that stranger, had he been of a remotely poetic mind, it would have been as if nature had inhaled massively, then sighed in relief to allow the earth to breathe freely once again. He would probably have said that the mood was overtly celebratory, that hope and relief had taken the November chill and warmed it into a summer glow.

Tommy was only conscious of the silence. The silence that he thought he had forgotten. A vacuum of sound that was not pillaged by the constant rattle of machine guns, the thundering explosions of shells, the report of a sniper's rifle or the scream of another victim of a trench mortar. Tommy heard a silence from death, and he was transfixed by its message.

They had all been made aware that the end was finally coming. It had been no secret that the machinations for peace were revolving. They had just not known exactly when or how it would manifest.

It arrived at 11 o'clock on 11th November.

As Tommy wandered transfixed by the quiet, he considered that moment just a short while ago when peace had been orchestrated.

The time; 11 o'clock.

The date; November 11. 11, 11, 11.

'Theatrical,' Tommy mused to himself. 11 on the 11th of the 11th. It was curious, he thought, that it should fall like that — almost as if it had been deliberately arranged, that the time and date had been chosen specifically for its beautiful numeracy simplicity. He thought it curious and also perhaps just a little unfathomable. 'Why had a ceasefire been called at all?' he questioned himself. It wasn't as if the war had been won, or even lost, by either side. The Germans had most definitely not been beaten back to Berlin and neither were the Allies drowning in the Channel. Far from it, they were instead all very much where they had always been, facing each other scant yards apart along broadly parallel trench lines that still stretched from the Belgian coast to Switzerland. Those lines of course had wavered and fluctuated over the years as each bite and hold had gained advancement for one army on the other. Each minor alteration, whether celebrated or mourned, was traced with great precision upon the huge maps lying on massive tables or hanging like tapestries on the walls in the glorious chateaus that housed the loudest and most commanding voices of both sides of the divide. The lines would become an almost incoherent smudge, an untidy annoyance. But for each irritation for the cartographer there had always been a corresponding, grotesquely disproportionate, haemorrhaging of the numbers written up by the regimental statisticians in their faintly lined ledgers.

No, Tommy thought, there was no victor. It was simply as if those in Paris, London, Washington or Berlin had simply come to the conclusion that enough was enough and it was now time to get back to the really important issues. Sport and fun had been had, everyone had put up an excellent show, but now there were more pressing items on the agenda, and it was time to move on. So, it was time to call a halt and declare peace, an armistice, and for such an auspicious achievement after all that had been suffered, a suitable and noteworthy time and date would of course be required. A time and a date that would be remembered and recorded for years to come, one that would remind future generations of the power of the Empire.

11 o'clock on the 11th day of the 11th month.

11.11.11.

Perfection!

Tommy was keenly aware that he ought to be celebrating the silence. That he should be drenched with the glow of optimism and hope. Relief should be flooding over his body from the simple knowledge that he had survived. The end had come, and he was there to greet it. He had crossed the line; he had made it.

Perhaps it was simply exhaustion that kept him from the exaltation, the total physical and mental fatigue of four years facing a hostile environment. More likely though it was the question that repeated constantly, spiralling through his mind.

Such a simple question for which he begged an answer. Had it all been worth it?

It tormented him.

Had it? Really?

All that they had gone through, all they had seen, all that they had done. Had it been worth it?

He glimpsed for a moment a face in front of him. The terror filled eyes of a boy. There were rivulets of blood flowing down the left cheek from a gash in the temple. The mouth was open, screaming and sobbing, but silently, as if fear was preventing sound from escaping. Tommy could sense the pleading, the begging to be spared, to be given a chance. And Tommy remembered himself in that moment. It was as if he was watching himself from a cinema seat in a filthy, flea ridden theatre where only the poorest, most desperate would purchase a ticket. The film flickered on the screen, but as he watched he could feel every movement that was made. His muscles tensing, his arms rising, pulling backwards, then plunging. He could feel the bayonet hit its mark. Every infinitely tiny moment of its journey was signalled from the blade to the rifle to the hands to the arms to the brain to Tommy's consciousness — the barely imperceptible popping of the eyeball, the cracking of the eye socket, the slicing through of the brain and the cracking of the skull like a goose egg. Then the sensory journey continued. He could feel the return of the weapon as it pulled back through the bone and blood and gelatinous body. But this journey was troubled with resistance.

To release the rifle of its burden he saw and remembered how he had to savagely kick the face away, in one final act of disrespect and disregard to humanity. As he watched he remembered how he had felt in that moment. In ignoring the plea and the terror he had passed out his judgment and punishment unhesitatingly, blankly and coldly. And in remembering, it made him sweat, made him panic and made him fear for his soul. For he had truly felt nothing. In the taking of a young life, he had felt nothing. No pity, no guilt, no remorse. He had been inhuman, a spectre of death that cared nothing for its victim and even less for himself. That was what the trenches had made him.

Now however that was all behind him, behind them all. That was the past and to be forgotten. The final whistle had been blown; transgressions would be forgotten. Now they could all go back to leading normal lives.

But could it return to normal? Tommy wondered. Could he return to normal? After what he had become, what he had seen and done, could he return to being a man? A normal, human, man? Could any of them? He sincerely doubted it.

Tommy remembered Railway Wood in the Ypres Salient. It was a glorious day with the sun high in the sky. The German guns were relatively quiet, and they were coming out of the front lines, traipsing slowly, but urgently and happily back towards the town and hence further behind the lines. They were all experienced now, experience came quickly in the trenches, so none of them had their guard down, they couldn't, especially in the Salient. But despite their caution, they still all felt a gentle sense of achievement. Once again, they had survived the front and their reward was a few days of relative safety behind the range of the German guns. Poperinge beckoned. Talbot House called out to them.

They were exhausted but half smiles were written on their grubby faces. They chattered sporadically between themselves, sometimes to themselves, about the joys that awaited them. The bath house, the stepping out of their louse infested uniforms, the Belgian beers, the cinema, the ladies that would release their tensions. If they could have lengthened their strides they would have done, but neither space nor energy allowed it. So, they were patient in their dreaming. They had all learnt patience in the trenches. It was the one thing that each and every one of them had learnt.

None of them picked up on the high-pitched whistle that heralded the chaos that was about to enshroud them as momentarily their senses had been lulled.

The panic and confusion were instantaneous and total.

From nothing the ground rocked violently, and they had all been shaken off their feet and thrown to the ground. But therein lay the confusion. They had felt the quake of the land around them, their bodies had responded automatically, and their instincts immediately recognised the shock of a landing shell. But as they lay sprawled and scattered their heads were all wracked with confusion. For all the motion and action, there had been no sound. There had been no great deafening explosion, there was no shower of destruction and body parts were not splayed amongst them. It was merely as if momentarily they were at the epicentre of a small, barely consequential earthquake.

For a moment or two the shock had silenced them, then there was a frantic checking of themselves, counting their own limbs, checking for wounds. Then their eyes surveyed the scene, as one mind counting the members of their company, verifying the continued existence of their mates. Then slowly they began to drag themselves back to their feet and universally seemed to shrug their shoulders.

Tommy had been projected forcefully backwards into something that once upon a time had been part of a hedgerow, his ankle twisting in the process. He shifted and felt a sharp stab of pain. He cursed his bad luck, an injury that was useless to him in every way. Clearly it was too slight an injury to be a blighty, to give him a ticket back home or indeed any meaningful release from service, but it was most definitely serious enough to cause him plenty of discomfort and grief in the ensuing days, and to make the march an agonising one.

He struggled slowly and awkwardly to his feet using his Lee Enfield rifle as a crutch and putting all his weight on the uninjured side. Slowly he raised his head to survey the spectacle around him. It was broadly comical. As his company battled with their packs and weapons it reminded him of a circus scene where all the clowns have dramatically thrown themselves to the ground to avoid being showered with water from an empty bucket, then attempting to regain their composure they battle with their oversized shoes and clothes.

Between his winces of pain Tommy was able to muster a smile. Then in his sweep of the scene his eyes fell onto Frank.

Frank was loved and ridiculed in equal measure by all in his Company. His appearance belied his best qualities and gave him the nickname of "Mole" which was used by everyone except by Tommy. No uniform ever fitted Frank properly, his short legs and rounded shoulders allied to his habitual shuffle rather than a march making it an impossibility. With his head inevitably angled to the ground his gait simply added to comic appearance. But it was Frank's passionate love of reading that completed the image that would ensure he was always a focus of some sort of ridicule as he was rarely without an open book with which he required spectacles to enjoy — spectacles that were small and round with thick lenses that when worn made his eyes appear like tiny pin pricks. Appointing him the nickname of "Mole" was the simplest and most unimaginative of actions.

Where Frank lacked poise and natural manly stature, he overcompensated in character and humanity. His generosity of spirit was always sincere, unquestioning and unhesitating, as ready to throw coins on the table for an extra beer as he was to take the heaviest load. He saw his time and energies and possessions not as his alone but to be shared freely with those that could use them better. Frank spoke little compared to many others who had less to say but when he did speak most listened and when he laughed all laughed with him. Not because he was the brightest or funniest of men, but because he was always the most sincere.

The night that Frank lost all of his enemies, all those that had ridiculed and tormented him relentlessly, was the same night that Arthur Cousins lost his leg.

That night a raiding party had been sent out deep into No Man's Land between the lines near Arras to glean whatever intelligence possible. Cousins, a rugby playing braggart had to be picked for the party, whilst Frank had volunteered unhesitatingly. Led by a young Lance Corporal, five of them in total crept out into the darkness of a moonless night that was lit only by the occasionally fired Very lights. They crawled and scraped their way over the pock-marked ground towards the thick tangle of barbed wire strewn between the trench lines and there found the narrow gap that gave them a route through to the German lines. Led by their officer, two of the party had passed through without incident when a Very light sparked into the night and illuminated the whole group. All five dropped from their stooping progression, flat to the ground instantly, hoping that if they could remain motionless, they would remain undetected by their enemy. But the Germans had been attentive, their lookouts had been concentrating and the sudden, mass movement was picked up. Within seconds Maxim guns raged into action and tore up the ground around the British men.

The Lance Corporal, the son of an ambitious local politician from the West Country, died in the manner that all parents were told their sons had died, instantly, bravely and facing the enemy. The shower of lead cut his body into fragments. Frank, who had been bringing up the rear of the group and had yet to get to the opening in the wire, was the most protected and had buried himself as much as he could in a shallow shell hole. Cousins, who was in front of him, panicked. He had been at the opening of the wire when the first hail of bullets sprayed out and had immediately raised onto his hands and knees, twisted his body back towards his own lines and then frantically tried to scramble homewards. His attempts to gain safety were still too slow. As the bullets spat all around into the mud, they made the wire weave, sway and finally lunge out to him. The wire seemed to grab Cousins and then envelop him. He screamed and struggled, flailing around trying to escape the barbs, but the more he moved, the more he was bitten into and the more the bullets were able to pick him out. His torment seemed to last an eternity in which bullet after bullet ripped into his leg.

The two men that had been between Cousins and their officer had been trapped within the thin corridor of wire. Their officer in front of them lay prone and still, behind them the struggle of Cousins was blocking their way and the bullets aimed at him in all his conspicuousness were biting. Stuck fast to the ground, with nowhere to go they felt the mud angrily flick up, the bullets searching them out.

Frank observed it all in his relative safety. He could quite easily have crawled back to his own lines and dropped into the trench praying loudly in thanks for his own safe return and for the hopeful return of his comrades. None would have judged him harshly; all would have accepted his self-preservation. But Frank's mind didn't work in that way. He saw what was happening in front of him and acted automatically. He crawled out of his safe space towards the wire.

Cousins was like a rabbit in a snare. His body dancing as he struggled and screamed from the enemy's torture. Frank got to him and grabbed his shoulders, pulling him closer to the ground, shielding him as much as he could with his own body. Frank said nothing but acted quickly and silently, clipping the wire that clung to Cousins with his cutters. Gradually, carefully and gently he freed the bigger man and pulled him out of the wire and then slowly dragged him as inconspicuously as he could to the parapet at the top of his own lines. Frank bundled the body of Cousins over the top and into the arms of the waiting men, then crawled back to where the rest of his group remained. Through the mauled gap in the wire, he found a way and grabbed the listless shoulders of the first man and pulled him through. It was a dead weight that felt limp and lifeless. Frank hoped that the soldier was just unconscious, but regardless he knew he still wanted to get him back to the confines of their own trench.

The bullets were gradually slowing in their intensity, rather than an unforgiving rain, they now sputtered sporadically but nevertheless were still deadly in their intent. For a second time Frank reached the top of the parapet and pushed over his charge, then once again twisted round and crawled back towards the wire.

Frank got all four men back and into the lines that night. The Lance Corporal's dead body being the penultimate one to drop over the parapet before Frank eased himself over and down. Neither of the two men caught between Cousins and the officer would survive the war, one died on the way to the casualty clearing station, his blood drained almost totally from his body, the other would last three more months before being buried in a mine explosion. Cousins' war was over that night. His bullet riddled leg would die and be lost, but the rest of him was saved and he would remain so when the guns fell silent.

Frank hadn't been uninjured. Twice the muscles in his right leg had felt the burning of lead and his forehead pounded with the furrow left by a bullet. But these were wounds that he would easily survive and put behind him, barely would he mention them and if they were ever brought into a conversation, he would make some joke about how he obtained them crawling from the enemy.

When Tommy's eyes settled on Frank, he felt that something was inherently wrong, but he couldn't calculate what. Frank was somehow propped up, neither quite standing nor quite sitting. His arms were flapping somewhat, and his hands seemed to search blindly for the spectacles that he kept in one of his top pockets. Frank's face was a portrait of shock and confusion, his eyes in a frenzy darting in every direction. Frank's tunic was pulled taut and save for a few new splashes of dirt was brushed and clean — even in the very worst of times Frank always took great pride in the appearance of his uniform, even if ultimately the uniform could never reciprocate by taking pride in the appearance of its wearer. As Tommy looked at Frank, he focused on the tunic. The tunic seemed to take up all of his vision. The tunic was now Frank, and Frank was now only the tunic, for where the tunic ended, so did he.

It was as if Frank was sat on the shell, like in a Bairnsfather cartoon and he had sailed into the trenches on it. But he hadn't. Where once he had a pelvis and legs, now he had a shell.

If that shell that now owned Frank had exploded as it should have done, and which it most definitely was intended to do, it would have destroyed most, if not all, of the company. For whatever reason it had chosen not to explode and so instead it had merely pierced Frank. As laughter began to ripple amongst the rest of the men, exalting in their shared luck, Tommy stumbled towards Frank. He grabbed his shoulder and Frank's head swivelled immediately to face him.

'Who's that? I can't see you. Who are you?'

'It's me Frank, just Tommy, you'll be fine, you've just got a bad 'un that's all.'

'Tommy? Thank God you're ok. I didn't know what happened. It just suddenly went dark, then it felt like I was pinned to the side.'

'It's fine Frank, you're fine, just covered in dirt, got a limber on you, I'll get you out. Just wait awhile.'

In the silence of the guns that surrounded Tommy now he could remember Frank clearly and he could sense those moments as if it was just seconds ago. Tommy remembered holding the dying man, just as he had held his own son so many times when he had woken frightened in the middle of the night. Tommy remembered the feel of Frank's shoulders, the weight of his head, the soft and fading voice that he had in those moments, sensing the man's life petering away, gradually leaving until, with one last great exhale the soul was released.

Tommy rubbed his face, squeezing his eyes together. Frank had been just one of the many that he had seen die in the noise of war. Now in the silence he began to see them all. The silence was pounding in Tommy's head, a thunderous, pulsating hammering that he couldn't escape. The silence was making him think and it was exhausting him more than any route march had ever done.

Tommy had never been a deep thinker. He had taken life pretty much as it had come. Good times, bad times, they had all just been accepted for what they were, nothing else. Now, middle aged, his youth behind him, it was as if his mind had started analysing his past and questioning his future. And in the silence of the guns, he kept asking himself the same question 'Had it all been worth it?'

Would Johnny Parr think that it had been worth it he wondered. That would surely be the clearest and simplest answer. If Johnny had felt it had been worth it, then it would have been.

Tommy had not known Johnny, but he knew his story. Johnny had been the first of them to fall over here. It would have been close to where he stood now, he thought, in Mons back in August, 1914. At fifteen years of age, Johnny had lied about his age to enlist two years before the war broke out, then at seventeen he would go to his grave to be remembered as the first of so many. How many others were there after Johnny? Tommy thought. It had to be more than hundreds or thousands, Tommy himself had seen hundreds die, probably it was tens of thousands or even hundreds of thousands, maybe even millions, he thought, He had no idea. But of them all, Johnny had been the first.

It wasn't always clear exactly what had happened to Johnny, some said that he fell on August 21, 1914 facing a forward advance of Uhlans. He had been with a small patrol on the outskirts of Mons when he spotted the advancing Germans.

'Go back and tell the rest of the boys,' he had told his patrol, 'I'll hold them off as long as I can.'

And he did hold them off, that's what they said, as long as

he could, until they got him. Until the Germans butchered him.

Others said that Johnny hadn't been killed by the Germans at all, that instead he had been shot by a panicking Belgian mistaking him for the advancing Hun. A case of "Friendly Fire". Tommy had heard both stories an equal number of times, but he hoped and wanted to believe that it was the Germans that had got him, that it had been a soldier's death. Whatever the truth, Johnny had been the first. The first of all of them.

So, what would Johnny think, Tommy asked himself for the countless time. Would he have thought it had been worth it? Losing his life here, only to know that four years later they would be right back at the same place, neither victors nor losers, but with so many others following in Johnny's footsteps into the dirt of Europe.

Tommy struggled with the thought, struggled to clarify his own opinion, struggled to reconcile himself against the notion that at this moment in time he should actually be celebrating the end of the war.

And what, Tommy's mind pressed him, would Johnny think if he knew that another, just like him, albeit a little older, had perished so close to the place where he had fallen, but over four years later in the dying hours of the war?

An hour and a half, maybe two hours previously, the news had spread like wildfire amongst all the ranks in the Mons sector, that while they waited for the silence, a Yorkshire lad serving in the Irish Lancers, George Ellison, had been shot dead by a sniper. Ninety minutes before the ceasefire some fuck of a Hun wanted to have the last word.

Tommy had known George, not well — they had all learnt that to survive in the lines they kept close friendships at arm's length — but he had known him well enough to drink with him, play Crown and Anchor with him, sing with him, share smokes with him.

George was a similar age to Tommy, he was in his late 30s at least but like all of them they wore their ages badly, he could have been older, 45 perhaps, 46 or 47. They had found themselves gravitating to each other in the scant few times that they had met, attracted subconsciously by their mutuality.

Both were old sweats who had served the Empire. Both reservists who had reenlisted on the outbreak of war, excited and energised with thoughts of regaining their youth and of having purpose and meaning again. Both of them were survivors. They had survived days and months and years of life on the Western Front, both had witnessed the dreadful, had committed the unthinkable, had experienced the worst. But they had survived.

Many of the young and naive serving with them had been lost, but Tommy and George had somehow continued to live and ride fate's fortune. Though they had both been inherently unlucky with the dice, they were relentlessly lucky with their lives, winning that roll of the dice day after day. Until this day. Until an hour and a half before the ceasefire would be confirmed at that all so special time of 11 on the 11th of the 11th. Some bastard of a German had taken aim and had made George the last of them to fall.

It had taken Tommy a while to fully disseminate the news of the killing. Death was such a part of life that the news wasn't news, until he reflected on the true futility of this particular sacrifice as the end of the war was clearly in sight. Then came the name. A familiar name, one he recognised but couldn't immediately put a face to. He had delved deeply into his memory trying to fit a name with a face. Then all of a sudden it was there. The handlebar moustache, ruddy complexion, scar above the left eye, big and solid hands, wide shoulders and a laugh that could rattle a barn. George Ellison. Yes, there he was, George. And now he was just another corpse.

The irony wasn't lost on Tommy. Each new dawn had seemed a little victory, a step closer to home. The ceasefire had opened the door tantalisingly to all of those still standing, they all had a hand on the handle, could smell the air of home, the taste of their wives' mouths, the grip of their children's hugs. George had stood on that threshold with all of them only for that door to slam in his face and eternity to grab him and propel him to whatever lay beyond. They hadn't been brothers or bosom pals, but they had connected, and the news of George had struck Tommy harder than most other losses.

At first it was as if his own rifle butt had struck him hard in the stomach, pushing out his air in an agonising exhalation. Then he had given out a laugh. A demonic like cackle at the cruelty and wickedness of it all. Then Tommy had just felt complete desolation. An emptiness of unfathomable magnitude. George's death was hard to take. His was truly a waste of a life. His felt like a murder.

So, had it all been worth it? God, the question revolved around Tommy's head.

Had Johnny Parr known that between him being the first and George being the last there were over four years of pain, countless being lost like them, but in distance hardly anything at all, would he, Johnny, have faced the enemy in the way that he was said to have done? Would he have sacrificed himself so nobly? Or would he have simply shrugged his shoulders, turned and left for home? Tommy just couldn't judge; he didn't dare to judge.

He stopped walking and looked around. He had been

wandering with little aim or direction, he hadn't any real idea where he was or how far he had gone from the rest of his battalion. But it didn't matter, it was more or less the same view everywhere. Mons was the mess of rubble like so many of the towns and villages they had known. It wasn't as bad as Ypres of course, nowhere could really compare with what Ypres had had to put up with, but it was still a desolate, soulless mess of broken homes and businesses. Barely a building stood untouched by the war, roads and streets were a shambles, gardens merged with one another as fences lay broken and splintered. Occasionally a rat would scamper from one dark recess to another, sometimes the evident quarry of a predatory cat. Nature had to some extent reclaimed the town, amongst the rubble the greenery of tenacious plants could be seen and in the sky with the silence of the guns prevailing, birds were voicing their presence, bringing harmony to the scene with their faultless melodies.

Tommy chose a wall that he could collapse on. It wasn't the exhaustion of recent exertions that sapped his strength, it was the toll of the many, many preceding months. He had been so strong for so long, but now his muscles were failing and he needed the wall. It was battered and weathered but there was an air of sturdiness about it and to Tommy it felt that he hadn't been given such a comfortable seat for years.

He allowed his eyes to blink slowly as he soaked up the relief his limbs were receiving. He held the blink longer and longer and then just let his eyes remain closed. Wonderful, dark, silent emptiness. His mind floated in the void for just a moment, then it pricked him like a thorn again and again and again, relentlessly asking him. Had it been worth it? Had it been worth it? Had it? Had it?

Had it?

What did he think? Forget about what Johnny would think, what did he think?

He kept his eyes closed and answered himself. Because the answer had been there, it had always been there. He had always known what he thought, though he wasn't always convinced that his was the right thought.

It had been worth it.

It was a hell of a price to pay — too high a price. One life was too high a price. Johnny's life alone was too high a price. But it will have been worth it. It must have been worth it.

When they signed up, when they all scribbled their names on those flimsy pieces of paper, they had done it for a multitude of reasons. But one single reason that prevailed amongst them all was the promise that they were given. A promise to them and to their families. It was, Tommy absolutely knew, that promise that would have made it all worth it.

'Fight for your God, your King and your Country', they had been coaxed. 'And when you come home again, we will give you a Land Fit for Heroes.' A land fit for heroes. That was the promise. Amongst all their other personal reasons, that was the one thing that each and every one of them had been fighting for.

A better country. A country of hope and opportunity, where there were more and better jobs, more equality. To create that country, will have made it all worth it. Tommy would unquestioningly lay down his life for that country, they would all have done. A country where their children and grandchildren and great-grandchildren could thrive and survive beyond the hardships that so many of them had grown and matured with. Tommy fought for the belief in the creation of a country that could truly be called Great Britain. He believed in it totally but had never envisioned that it would come at such a cost.

Tommy's fingers delved into his top pocket and pulled out his tobacco. Though he sometimes lit up or shared a fag, he had never taken to cigarettes in the same way that most others did, he had never felt a bond with them, they were too casual in their acquaintance, things that were just used and then thrown away. His pipe however had been a constant friend that he could turn to repeatedly, a warm comfort that soothed his gossiping mind and surrounded him in a sweet protective cloud.

He closed his eyes again as he brought the smoke down deep into his lungs, holding it there like an internal blanket for a moment. Then he released it and surveyed the town. Very flares were being sent up into the midday light, their colours and glow diluted by the sun but their message of hope and celebration clear in their presence. Could he really be going home? Would he really soon be back in the arms of his darling Alice?

Lovely, precious Alice.

He could never fathom what he had ever done to deserve such a blessed creature as Alice? She was simply perfection in his eyes, and had been since the very first moment that he had seen her. It was an instant attraction, a fairy tale intoxication.

He had been sitting in a coffee house in Crystal Palace dressed in the uniform that he loved with some free days to spare. Even in his own time he preferred to wear his service uniform, he enjoyed the doffing of caps from gents passing by, the comments and pointing of young children and the flirtatious smiles from the ladies. It was a uniform that hadn't as yet seen a great deal of experience, just like its wearer it hadn't yet witnessed the heat of battle or travelled from the shores of Britain, but there had been talk that the Boers were causing a nuisance and that soon both uniform and owner could be sent to sort the situation out. Tommy's young mind had been thrilled with the thought of a fight, each day waking with excited anticipation that this would be the special day that he would be given his orders. That morning he had woken with the usual hope that it was to be a special day. And it was to be. Though not because of any far-off projected conflict.

He had washed and dressed as usual and then decided to utilise his free time by a saunter through the municipal gardens. It was an overcast day, but the air was still warm and there was barely a breeze. He soaked up the casual attentions of strangers and then eventually decided it was time for some refreshment. He bought himself a Standard from a boy with a shrill and irritating voice and walked into the coffee house that he had known well before he had taken the King's shilling. Tommy took a chair at a small circular table, opened up his newspaper and began to pick out the articles that piqued his interest.

He was proud of his reading; he could read well for someone who had never had a proper schooling as his mother had been insistent that he learnt and that he practiced. Each night from when he was first able to comprehend as a toddler until he ventured out into the man's work-place as a twelve-year-old, his mother would sit him down and teach him the best way she knew how. It started with simple pictures that she made out of letters with chalk on slate, words like "bed" with the "b" being the headboard and the "d" the bedstead and "cat" with the "c" becoming a face with eyes and whiskers and the "t" a feline tail. Her lessons were always a game. Then in time he was able to read by himself the stories that were shared from neighbour to neighbour, usually simple pamphlets with line drawings as illustrations. He would read everything and anything that came his way with a voracious appetite. Sometimes the stories were in keeping with his youth and imagination, boys' stories of Empire adventures with the redcoats defeating Napoleon's forces, other times the things he read filled him with dread and fear, lurid accounts of murder and mayhem in the very backstreets of London where he lived. As an eight-year-old these tales would often become his nightmares. But as he grew and gradually saw and appreciated more of the world in which he lived the stories lost their personal threat, but never their thrill. The pamphlets and rare books that he obtained, became a huge part of his world, an escape that he could turn to whenever the damp and cold of the two rooms that he shared with his mother, became less than their home.

His mother had told him from an early age that reading, and writing, weren't just an escape for his imagination, but were also an escape from the poverty that he had grown up with. Literacy was his ladder out and he had to treasure it and be proud of it.

Though there had been a lack of wealth in Tommy's childhood, a lack of warmth in the cold wet winters and often a lack of food, Tommy had always been a happy boy and if quizzed later on in life, would always say that it was an idyllic childhood. His mother had loved him from the day that he was born, and he had never for one moment doubted that love. She worked slavishly to pay the rent, to put food on the table and to put clothes on their bodies and hardest of all, to give them time to share together. Tommy was her life and she illustrated it to him in every tiny detail of her day.

It was never easy for her to bring in the pennies, especially when Tommy was tiny, but she did whatever she could. She may have been poor, but she was never dirty and at times had held down positions as a salesgirl, a maid and eventually, when Tommy was able to help her, she had saved up enough of those precious pennies to invest them in a barrow to sell fruit and vegetables at Covent Garden Market. Her literacy had always been, in her mind, her one strength and if she were to give her son one gift it was always going to be that he would never be mistaken for an idiot.

She wasn't unusual in her hardships. The country cared little for those at the edges of society. They remained largely overlooked and were left to survive in the best way that they found possible. But she was perhaps unusual in her tenacity and self-worth. She had escaped a childhood of abuse in rural Wiltshire with the arrival of a sweet-talking Welshman. A charming salesman that made decent money from transporting simple women's fashions to the rural communities. Seventeen years her senior she was beguiled by his confidence, his easy manner and the way he held court with every young, and not so young, woman that perused his wares. Many gave up their hard-earned pennies to him, plenty gave him more than coins and would then float around the village, heads held high, proud that he had plucked their feathers.

Tommy's mother was not one of those girls. Though at sixteen she was younger than most of them she was wiser and more cunning and had her eye on a greater prize than a moment under the Welshman's blankets. He was her escape, and she was going to make him want her more than anything he had wanted in his life. The treasure that she possessed would have to be hard earned and won by him, not given up cheaply for a piece of cut cloth.

The seduction was, for her, easy. Young flesh normally came without effort to him, even with the years under his belt, so to come across a near-child who showed little interest in him, who didn't giggle stupidly at his jokes and who wasn't interested in the compliments he showered on her, tantalisingly peaked his

31

desire. She became the prize that he was determined to win and one which he was determined he would win. He lavished gifts on the girl and began to make his intentions evident. She soon knew that she had him firmly fixed onto her line, she could reel him in at will.

With a maturity and instinct belying her years she toyed with the Welshman. She would tease with a smile and a cursory glance the one day and then ignore him entirely the next. Blow a kiss and giggle in one moment, then sneer and toss her head disdainfully the next. The girl was an enigma that he couldn't decipher and in so being she became all that he had ever desired.

When she was finally convinced that she had won him she gently pulled the line with a flutter of her eyelashes, a casual touch of her hand and the showing of a bare shoulder.

Then she pulled the hook tighter by scoffing at his accent and putting down his petty wares, and then finally, as he desperately offered her the prettiest of lace bodices as an extravagant gift, she secured her prey with a sudden, unexpected quick, hard, hot kiss on his lips. Even with his age and experience he was taken by surprise. He gasped involuntarily and even felt his knees buckle. Then she giggled casually, grabbed her new gift and turned on her heels, swishing her skirts as she walked away from him.

From that moment the Welshman was hers and her escape tunnel was dug and shored up.

That one kiss had given him an insatiable desire for more and he made it perfectly clear to her that his ardour was for her and her alone, but that first solitary kiss was all she was prepared to offer him. That, and the occasional words of affection laced with a caustic sarcasm that variably questioned his manhood or ridiculed his age. Any other touches or gifts that she may or may not have been prepared to give would simply have to wait.

It had taken her a little over six months from the first time the Welshman had visited the village to the time that he wouldn't leave without her. Then finally, without a word to her parents, her family or her friends she packed a simple bag and left with him early one morning.

Her previous life, her childhood and all her dark memories she left behind as she put her hand into his. She was firmly and forever closing the door on the demons that had been at her night window or in her bed. Now, another life stretched in front of her and whatever it held, it couldn't and wouldn't be worse than the one she was leaving.

There was no doubt in her mind that she had fallen for him. The charms that worked on most of the girls he wanted had also worked on her. She, however had always maintained her composure and self-discipline and refused to allow him to be the seducer. She was resolved and determined never to succumb to his pressures, nor her own desires, until her chain was wrapped firmly and unequivocally around him.

The chain was locked in a small, half-forgotten chapel with only a near toothless spinster, a local farmhand and the minister to bear witness.

To him the ceremony was a means to an end, a casual promise to reap the pleasures of all that her young body proffered. To her it was a moment of delight and release, an allowance to herself that she could relax, she had escaped, but beyond that she had become the princess in her own fairy tale. Finally, she felt as if she had been whisked away by a gallant and noble prince and night after night, she gave her body and soul to him in complete supplication and adoration. Her happiness was fulfilled.

As they travelled, they often appeared to the world as father and daughter, but in her vision, she was a woman secured to her man. A man that would care for her and love her and give her the life for which she had always craved.

His home was on the English side of the Welsh Borders, a cold, soulless building upon which she gradually imprinted a femininity. When at the end of their first six months she felt the first touches of life growing within her she felt that her own existence had been fulfilled and the home she had been creating consequently began to become her nest.

Two months later he asked her to stop accompanying him on his business trips and then, when her term was coming to a close, she discovered for the first time the true quality of the man she had married.

At first, she would excuse the abuse, blaming it on the alcohol she now realised he was so fond of. But his words still bit deeply into her heart and wounded her far more profoundly than the strikes on her body and face.

One evening she dared to question his late return, then the unmistakeable smell of another's musk on his body. His response was instant and merciless, first he lashed out with his tongue, then he thrust a fist hard into her belly.

Her self-confidence evaporated in that instant and for the first time in her life she felt a real sense of terror. A fear not simply of danger to herself but of harm to something that already meant more to her than her own life, the tiny child that was growing within her.

She had been no stranger to fear and abuse, they had been constant companions for much of her life, but her heart had never been truly threatened by anyone before and evil, she felt, had never deceived her. But in that moment her trust in herself and in her own instincts dissipated and she felt totally broken and vulnerable.

And yet she excused him and forgave him, and she held on to hope.

Her forgiveness was charitable and her optimism in vain as the extent of his personality revealed itself. Often, he would be the charmer she had fallen in love with and whom she was happy to share a bed with. Other times he was a brainless thug who was liberal with both his physical and mental violence, leading her to spend unsleeping nights, with a meat knife gripped firmly in her fingers under a pillow. Then other times he was a child, a pathetic, weeping urchin that begged for forgiveness, love and support.

Whichever creature walked through her door she learned to identify in an instant and to quickly adapt and relate to. Who she had become, she had no idea.

She was fortunate that there were those around that knew of his traits and looked for signs of her well-being. The closer she came to unburdening her load, the more that friendly faces would appear at the door or tap gently on a window. When the time came, she had her support, but not from her man. Whether she knew or guessed or didn't care that he was in another's wife when she was lying screaming with the effort of bringing life into the world, she wouldn't reveal. Kind and aged hands held hers, cracked but wise voices calmed her fears and Tommy arrived, bloody but healthy.

As Tommy nourished himself for the first time, she found a cause that would truly fulfil her life.

She never wanted or intended Tommy to grow up without a father. She felt, instinctively, that a man in his life was what was needed and she could put up with all the difficulties that were thrown at her for the sake of her son. Her mind was changed one night, shortly after Tommy had unknowingly passed his first birthday.

Tommy's father returned to the home that she had made after four days away. He was sober but his mind was plagued with jealousies and fury. Words were being spat in a blaze from his lips before he had even opened the door and entered the room. She saw the fire in his eyes and immediately grabbed Tommy up from the fire hearth where a solitary woodlouse had been entertaining him and she enveloped him in a protective shield of loving arms. Her man's tongue lashed at her, stabbed at her, swiped at her, but there was no substance to his accusations, and she knew it wouldn't last. She guessed that one of his tarts had found someone other than him to lie down with and it was that that was causing his upset.

But he wouldn't be calmed. Turning her back to him infuriated him more. With Tommy screaming in her arms, he grabbed her hair and threw her to the floor. A stack of kindling saved her head from anything more serious than lacerations and bruises, but blood still flowed freely. Tommy knew nothing other than distress and his wails resonated deafeningly round the room. His father picked him up and tossed him carelessly into the cushions of an armchair. Then stood above his woman. Surveyed her. Spat on her and then hauled her to her feet with his hands once again around her blond locks. She had little choice. Her head swam with confusion and pain and her feet stumbled where they were directed. He forced himself upon her in a way that he had never done before.

After it was over, she refused to weep, though her eyes burnt with the desire. She lay at his side like a discarded toy and waited for his breathing to slow. Then she eased herself from the bed and on shaking legs crept back to her son.

She felt utterly helpless, and it terrified her, but what scared her more was the flippant and casual way in which the monster had tossed his own son away.

She sat with Tommy, cradling him in her arms, desperately trying to coax some confidence into both of their bodies. She stared into the glowing embers of the fire, her torn clothes barely covering her, and resolved to find a new life for herself and her son.

The man she had married, was no man, no hero, no knight, he was monstrous and pathetic, and he would never be a fit father to her son. If she remained with him, then she would be failing her son just as much as she would be failing herself. Whilst he snored gutturally on the bed, spent from his exertions, she made her plans.

For two weeks she quietly waited for him to leave on his business travels all the time concocting plans in her head. When the time finally came and he kissed her goodbye it was with an ignorance that when he would return three days later, both his wife and his son would be gone.

She hadn't been rash or foolhardy, but she had acted quickly. She had no money that she could call her own, but she felt no tug at her conscience in taking half of the cash that he had stashed away in the tin kettle that stood idly above the stove. Tommy, after all was his son and she was his mother, they were due a helping hand. Her share came to a little under £5, which wasn't a fortune, but it was nothing to be sniffed at and would give them both a start and a chance.

Her plan was a simple one, she would walk to Monmouth with Tommy in her arms, find the train station and from there head to London. Once reaching the capital she had no further plan, she just trusted in her own abilities to cope and survive.

The night before they were to leave seemed unending. Her mind battled to cover every eventuality, every excuse that she would have to make if he caught her halfway to freedom, every defence she would have to make against his violent recriminations.

He left as dawn appeared and with the closing of the door behind him, she took a deep breath and disciplined herself to hold back from doing anything other than that which would be normal for her at that time of day, just in case he had forgotten something and returned. She cleaned out the hearth, washed the breakfast bowls, washed and dressed Tommy, and tidied the bed sheets back into place. For two hours she did nothing but the usual, then, satisfied that he wasn't coming back, she flew her plan into action.

Years later she would recall that it was the journey to Monmouth that was the hardest to bear. In her arms Tommy soon became a leaden weight and the sun, though hardly blazing, melted her with every step. She had underestimated how long it would take them and how much food and water they would require. Before they had travelled for three hours, with little over half the distance covered she was exhausted. Each step had become a trial and more and more frequently she had to rest, leaning on a low wall or propped against a tree trunk. Tommy dutifully slept most of the time, oblivious to the change his life was making and the change of his surroundings. When he woke it was because he was hungry, or because his body expelled that which it didn't need, and it was irritating him with discomfort. Each time, they would stop again, he would feed or be cleaned, and she would delve into the provisions she had grabbed, provisions that very soon seemed meagre and desperately insubstantial.

She kept each rest as short as she was able, then she would pull herself back to her feet, arrange her pack, take Tommy into her arms and make the first step of the next little section, always conscious of the dread that she felt, the fear that he would discover their disappearance too soon and would chase them down on the road. Constantly she could imagine his fingers round her throat, squeezing the life out of her body. So, she walked, rested and walked again, gradually eating up the miles. She was nothing if not tenacious and each step was a step further from him, and with each step the fingers round her throat began to loosen. It was undoubtedly her journey of a thousand miles, if not in distance, in mental strength.

When Monmouth finally began to show itself on the horizon, she felt a burst of energy flush through her veins and for a while, twenty minutes or so, her pace quickened, then her muscles complained too much and she slowed to the speed that would at least get her to her destination. Monmouth loomed larger and larger, it called to her, encouraged her. She shrugged away her aching limbs, put her head down and trudged. The promise of a port to a new existence was her fuel.

Tommy would never know his father and would never know of how his mother had laboured to take them from his grip. He wouldn't remember the rural backwaters that had once been his home, his childhood memories would always be of London with its busy streets and alleyways. Memories of a mother who never failed him, always gave him everything that she was able, showered him with love and security, but who equally never hesitated to discipline him when necessary. Few had little material worth in the streets that Tommy would grow up in, but Tommy would grow up with everything that he would ever need.

As Tommy turned a page of his newspaper, patiently waiting to be served, his eye caught a movement at the tables nearby. His eyes left the newspaper and followed the movement. It was just a girl, the waitress taking orders. He looked back at his paper, but then looked up again. There was something about this girl, something that commanded his attention. He watched her casually, intrigued by his own interest. She was attractive, he judged, but no more so than many of the girls he had known. A nice face that had a ready smile and laughing eyes, not heart-stoppingly beautiful, just pretty. There was a poise and grace in her movements, a serenity, but she was no ballet dancer, she just moved nicely. What was it, he asked himself? Something. Just something.

Suddenly the girl turned her head, and her eyes met his. It was as if she could feel his gaze boring into her and wanted it to stop. Her fingers were still holding her pencil and it was scribbling on the pad in her left hand, she was listening and taking heed of the order of the couple at the table she was at, but she was looking straight at him. Her smile melted, she glowered and Tommy, with his cheeks reddening dived back into his paper and became engrossed in an advert. After a minute or two, as he felt his colour lightening, he sensed the girl walk past his table. He didn't look up, but he felt that she was scowling at him and her steps sounded brisk and cross.

She returned to the table with a small tray bearing a teapot with cups and saucers. Tommy risked a casual glance up and once again felt a certain enchantment with the girl. With the newspaper acting as a weak shield, he watched and observed her, listened to the few words that came from her lips. She had an inner beauty. Perhaps Tommy was the only one that could see it, he certainly didn't understand why no-one else was watching her as he was, maybe he was the only one with the special sight. But he could certainly see it and the more he watched, the better and clearer he could see it, it was almost glowing from her skin. It was a beauty that he had only ever felt before, never seen, a beauty that had been his mother's soul.

Tommy was entranced by the girl and although he held the newspaper as if he was engrossed, his eyes couldn't leave her even for a second as she glided from one table to another taking and delivering orders.

After a while he grew more confident in his observations and whenever she happened to turn in his direction and catch his eyes, as she most certainly did, he ventured a smile and then even a friendly wink. Nothing that he did however caused her to do anything but look through him or stare coldly. He knew his attempts at flirtation were clumsy and gauche, what he couldn't work out was whether they were being noticed at all. What he was keenly aware of was that whether from intention or accident she never came to his table to take his order though she came to all of those around him and he ended up spending the rest of the morning thirsty and just a little bit hungry. He eventually left without having any of his growing appetites satisfied.

Tommy was troubled for the rest of the day with images of the girl. She followed him through the park, peered up to him from his evening broth and looked down on him as he lay in bed at night. He was simply enchanted, and he resolved to do something about it.

He returned to the cafe the next morning and sat at the same table. This time he had no newspaper, he was going to make it clear that he wanted attention and would grab it if he had to. She appeared like the day before, a vision in his eyes that glided from table to table, but never to his own. His eyes watched her every move, urging her to change direction and head for him. He played with the condiment set on the table, coughed conspicuously and rocked on his chair, but still he was kept waiting. Then, she strode purposely towards another of the girls working the tables. There was a nudge, some words and a glance to his table, then a nod from the other girl. A minute later Tommy was being asked for his order, but not from the one that had become mistress of his attention.

Tommy returned to the cafe the next day, and the day after that, in the vain hope of being able to talk to the girl but she avoided him on every occasion, with other, less attractive propositions taking his orders and relieving him of his pennies. Finally, the day came when, with no other patrons and no other waiting staff, she had no choice but to approach his table.

She stood in front of him, starchily erect, her face blank with disinterest, challenging him to ask her for anything other than a beverage or cake. He stuttered out a request for a pot of tea and left it at that. Momentarily she felt disarmed by his apparent lack of confidence but gave no hint that she felt nothing other than disdain for the soldier.

The following day she found herself looking out for him, checking the clock in the corner and peering out of the window. Then when he appeared and pushed open the cafe door, she felt a surprising warm jump in her stomach. A few minutes later she made a beeline for his table.

Even then she was not overtly friendly, but she did condescend to offer a small smile, and when he asked her name, she replied unhesitatingly.

'Alice.'

'Well, Alice,' Tommy responded. 'My name is Tommy, and I'm very pleased to know you.' From that moment they were friends, he visited the cafe day after day but ensured that he stayed only long enough for a brief drink and a few short conversational sentences in which he aimed at the very least to entice a smile from her if not a small laugh. Alice warmed daily to her admirer.

After a week of small talk, feeling that the time was right, Tommy mustered enough courage to ask the question that he wanted to ask since the first day that he had seen her.

'Lovely day today Alice,' he began.

'It is Tommy,' she answered' 'Especially for this time of year, when it can often be so drizzly.'

'I wonder if I may ask you a question Alice?' he stretched the words out as he felt his skin warm and panic slowly rise within him, this was the moment, it was make-or-break, and he was desperate for it not to be break.

'Yes, I suppose so,' she replied.

'Alice, I wonder if... I mean to say... well, do you think... well, might it be possible... sometime... it doesn't matter when of course... just one day perhaps... would you perhaps...'

'Oh, for goodness sake Tommy, what are you trying to say? You sound like an imbecile.' Alice stopped him, instinctively she knew exactly what he was trying to verbalise and her resistance was utterly defeated by his awkwardness and nervousness.

'If you are trying to ask if I will take a walk in the park with you, then quite simply the answer is not bleeding likely,' she fired at him sternly.

'Oh, oh, right, ok, well that was it, but of course, of course, absolutely.' He stammered, completely shell-shocked and crushed by her words.

'Not bleeding likely,' she repeated. 'Whilst you insist on wearing that flaming uniform of yours. I wouldn't want people thinking that I only walked out with a boy because he was a soldier. Haven't you got some gentleman's clothes? Anything other than that.' She pointed aggressively at his uniform, a frown on her face.

'Um, well yes of course I have, I just thought that, well that, well that this is what...'

'What girls wanted?' she interrupted crossly. 'You think that as long as you're wearing your uniform that you can have any girl that you set your eyes upon, don't you? That they'll just swoon over you and grab your arm. Well mister, that is not how it works for this girl,' she poked herself in the chest. 'I am not interested in any uniform, so don't even think of asking me to take a walk with you until you can find something else to wear.' With that she angrily turned on her heel and stomped back towards the kitchens.

Tommy felt that he had just suffered a greater tongue lashing than anything a sergeant major had thrown at him and he was utterly perplexed. Clearly, she had rebuked him but there was also that subtle implication that under the right conditions she was actually prepared to walk out with him.

The following day he turned up at the cafe for the first time wearing the only other clothes he possessed, a well-worn, but still respectable brown wool suit with a flat cap on his head. Alice beamed inwardly when she saw him, but she was not about to lose the ground that she had made. She waited a while before she finally sauntered to his table, her head down all the time supposedly reading her notepad.

'Good morning sir, may I take your order?' she questioned not looking up, her stomach fluttering with anticipation.

'Alice it's me, Tommy.'

She looked up quickly, 'Oh Mr Atkins, I'm sorry I didn't

recognise you. How are you today? Well, I hope. Have you decided on your order?'

'Mr Atkins?' Tommy replied with a note of exasperation. 'Mr Atkins?' he repeated. 'What's wrong with you Alice? It's Tommy, it's always been Tommy, not bleeding Mr Atkins.'

'Oh, I'm so sorry to cause offence sir,' she took up. 'It's just you look so much more... more...' She searched for the word, 'more mature, now that you're not wearing that silly uniform.' She flashed a wickedly teasing smile at him, then went on, 'the usual, is it? Pot of tea? And how about a nice cake to go with that?'

'Alice!' Tommy expostulated. 'What has gotten into you?'

'Tea?' she questioned again.

'Yes, bleeding tea.' He replied crossly.

'Cake?'

'No, I do not want any bleeding cake!'

'Really sir, there is no need for that kind of language here.'

'Alice!' he implored desperately.

'Yes?'

'Stop it.'

'Stop what sir?'

'Stop all this nonsense. I thought you'd like me like this.'

Alice held her breath. The silence enveloped them both for a moment that seemed to go on forever, then so quietly she whispered, 'I do Tommy. I like you very much like that.'

Tommy slumped in his chair, the emotion of the exchange exhausting him. 'Then, why are you behaving like, like... this?'

'Like what?' Alice asked still whispering, the faintest of smiles on her lips.

'Like this Alice,' Tommy replied.

'As I explained, Mr Atkins, you appear... different to me

today…'

Tommy began to comprehend the game that Alice was playing with him. All along he had felt that he was the pursuer and she the pursued, now he realised it was totally a game of cat and mouse and he was the one that was squeaking.

'Alice?' he started earnestly.

'Yes?'

'Would you take a walk with me some time?'

'Of course, I will, I thought you'd never ask,' she beamed into his eyes.

Their subsequent courtship was a relatively slow and controlled affair. Tommy wasn't particularly confident around the fairer sex and Alice's attitude to him had done nothing to improve that confidence. Alice however revelled in taking control of the romance. The arrogance that she had originally perceived in the young soldier winking at her had been replaced with a humbleness that she found irresistible. With each venture out together her trust in Tommy increased and their mutual attraction was enhanced. After two weeks in which a day had not gone by without them seeing each other, Tommy ventured to plant a kiss on the young girl's cheek, Alice accepted it nonchalantly, but with her stomach tying itself in knots. A further two weeks later Tommy had suggested they sit themselves down on a bench for a while to watch the swans gliding over the lake. It was an autumn afternoon, and the leaves were already beginning to fall, the air was dry, but a breeze was whipping around them.

'It's a little chilly Tommy, can't we keep walking?' Alice responded to his suggestion.

'Please Alice, just for a moment, just so that we can watch the birds,' he insisted.

'But I'm cold Tommy, can't we watch them as we walk round?'

'Alice, please,' he implored.

'Oh, very well, but not for long, we'll catch our death if we're not careful.'

They sat down, Alice making it perfectly clear that she was doing so begrudgingly. Then they both stared out onto the lake. Alice made a show of pulling her coat closer around her and blew long and loudly into her cupped hands. Tommy ignored her, lost in his own mind.

'Is that long enough?' Alice asked.

'Just a moment more Alice,' he answered.

'It really is quite cold Tommy.'

He ignored her, then in a sudden movement turned and grabbed her hand. The quickness of the action surprised her and she automatically slid to the end of the bench. Then, without loosening his grip he dropped from the seat to his knee.

'Good gracious Tommy, what are you doing? You'll ruin your trousers,' she responded, quite confused by what he was doing.

Tommy raised his face to look into her eyes. His voice quivered slightly as he spoke.

'Alice my dear, my love, although I am just a ne'er-do-well soldier, will you consent to marry me? Will you be my wife?'

Alice gasped, half in surprise at the question and half in surprise at Tommy's initiative. Her mouth opened to speak, then it snapped shut. Her forehead frowned and momentarily there was a flash of annoyance in her eyes that made Tommy recoil. She turned her head away from him and held it there for the most agonising of seconds, but her hand she left in his. Then, finally, she turned back to him and with a face creased with happiness and a small tear glistening in her eye she answered him.

'Mr Atkins, whether you wear the uniform of a soldier or anything else, I would be proud to marry you and call myself your wife.'

Tommy leapt up, dragging her to her feet with him, threw his arms around her and kissed her in the way he had dreamt about since he had first seen her.

They were married the following month in a small ceremony. Tommy had two members of his company present, Alice had her parents, sisters and older brothers with her. They spent their first night as a married couple in a small room above an inn, then the following day Alice moved her few, simple possessions into the lodgings that Tommy called home.

For a month their life together was a romantic idyll. In between her work at the cafe and his duties they spent every minute together, savouring each other's presence, lost in their love. In the fifth week of marriage their bliss was curtailed when he was given notice that he was being sent to South Africa to help in the conflict with the Boers.

As Tommy now sat on the wall in the ruins that was Mons, it was that first, heavenly month with Alice that he was thinking about. He could feel the gentle whisper of her hands in his — hands that were blessed with wispy, thin pianist's fingers that could barely, even then, wrap around his stubby, scarred and swollen palms. Her quiet and calm voice was in his ear giving words of comfort and support spoken with the fairest of breaths. Tommy could sense her lips passing over his and then almost imperceptibly showering his cheeks, eyes and forehead with dainty tokens of affection. And in his arms, he could imagine her slight weight, the ease and joy of picking her up, grabbing her and holding her tightly. For these wonderful moments of imagination, they were both young again. He was untainted by the last four years and she was innocent from grief. They were just as they had been in that wonderful first month and every ounce of his being ached to return to that time so that even for just a fraction of a moment, he could have everything returned that he had lost or had been stolen from him.

Of course, he wanted that "Land Fit for Heroes" that they had been promised, the country that would offer them all a better future, but most of all, in that second, in that breath, all he really wanted was to be back in the arms of his dear, lovely, precious Alice. Safe. Loved. Protected. Needed.

He didn't know how long he remained there. In his thoughts. In repose. But he was cold when his mind returned to the present and his back and legs ached from lack of motion. It was darker, but it wasn't yet dusk, and the silence of the guns could still be heard.

He pulled himself slowly to his feet, buttoned up his great coat and picked up his Lee Enfield, looked around and guessed the direction back to his company. Then slowly he walked with his mind back in the present and the protective shield raised once more around his heart and thoughts to ensure that however many days remained for him in khaki and on the Western Front, he would survive them intact so that he could finally return to his angel and hold her in his arms once again.

PART 2
LONDON
November 1922

For almost four years they had been back home, those who had been lucky enough to be returned first. Four years. And what had they got? Nothing! When they had stepped off the ships onto the hallowed ground of Dear Old Blighty, they had done so with relief and excitement, anticipation and optimism. They had survived in one form or another and they were stepping home to claim their prize. A prize long promised and much talked about. They were the victors, they were the returning heroes, they were the generation that would be glorified for their exploits and sacrifices. Everything that they had seen or done in war, they would be able to put behind them to be reborn into the New World Order that would be Britain. They all knew it and they all believed in it. It was their destiny and theirs to enjoy.

But those hopes and beliefs hadn't lasted. As the celebrations to returning heroes ebbed quietly away, reality and truth slowly seeped back into their lives.

Tommy didn't step through the doorway to his home until March of the year after the Armistice and already he was a broken man. Influenza had torn like a wildfire throughout Europe. Those that had been weakened and wounded from their time in the trenches had fallen in their droves, but so had whole populations of civilians far from the sounds of reporting guns. Whatever annihilations had transpired on the sun and shell-cracked ground in the Somme Valley of 1916, the Spanish Flu was making it pale in comparison, millions upon millions were falling in the pandemic.

Tommy had escaped the virus. It hadn't been through any great effort on his behalf, he had just been lucky. For whatever reason, he didn't get afflicted, he hadn't fallen victim. But Tommy did witness the deadly trail that the disease had scored through the camps, towns and villages through which he passed. So often he felt that he followed in its wake, sometimes feeling that he was days and weeks behind it, other times just hours or even minutes. Wherever it had been the destruction was no less than he had experienced on the battlefields, except the chaos that remained after the virus' surge was not a pock marked landscape and derelict buildings as the shells on both sides had created, but a dark silence that was only punctuated by the tragic tears of the mourners.

As Tommy strode amongst those communities that had been ravaged by the disease, his thoughts were always only of returning home. He imagined himself opening his front door. The warmth would hit him and blanket him. The glow of the fire in the hearth would beckon him in and he would be enveloped by the smell of freshly baked bread. He would step over the threshold and Alice would be there. She would turn at the sound of the door latch rising. Instinctively her hands would go to her head and gently smooth down her hair. By the time she saw who was returning she would be untying her apron strings. Tommy imagined that he would be a surprise to her, that she would only be expecting to see a sister or perhaps a neighbour. The sight of him would make her issue an involuntary scream. Her hands would shoot to cover her mouth and then her eyes would well up with tears. Only then, as realisation dawned that he was truly standing in their home would she allow herself to believe the truth, she would run to him, throw herself at him, on him and around him. It would be the welcome that every returning serviceman craved and looked forward to and it engrossed Tommy's mind.

The images of his return home fuelled every day of his life and put energy into each step. When he was eventually given the date on which he would be released from service it seemed to him such a long time ahead, such was his growing impatience, but in reality, it was a scant few days.

Each day brought him closer to his wife. He was moved to the Belgian coast, then sent back over the Channel and barracked at Folkestone. The proximity was tantalising and frustrating, there were still duties that he had to perform, he could only go when they told him he could go.

It was the day before he was to be released that he received the short letter from his sister-in-law, Alice's youngest sister. It was a sensitive note, but brief and to the point. The details were scant and without flourish but told how the flu had struck Alice, how she had then battled it bravely, full on and without complaint. It said how Alice had been determined that her Tommy should not know that she was ailing. She had fought it for almost three weeks as if it were her own personal Passchendaele. But each passing day hadn't been another day simply survived, another day closer to the objective, it was rather another day that had weakened her and sapped her of her strength and belief.

Finally, Alice had succumbed.

Tommy had read the note quietly, alone on the cliffs above the town. The words immediately stunned every part of his being. Where he had minutes before been a man with hopes and dreams, he was now a vacuous vessel devoid of all that gave his life meaning. He read the note again in the hope that the words would change, that perhaps he had misunderstood or misread something. Nothing changed in the wording. He was paralysed with an overwhelming wave of grief. He looked at the sea but saw nothing. Then he wept. He wept, and he wept, and he wept.

The following day, broken beyond all belief, Tommy headed back to the house that he had called home knowing that his life was lost. He wouldn't even have the closure of being at Alice's side as they lowered her into the ground, that had all been done. All that awaited him was a cold and empty shell of a building.

For four years now he had lived alone, taking each day as it came with his sole ambition to get to the end of another twenty-four hours. It was an existence, nothing more. He wasn't alone, wherever he went he could see the same depression that was molesting him was also gripping others. Even for those who came back to held out arms and warm fires, there was still a clear malaise. Darkness gripped the country.

The desolate days had turned into weeks, then months and eventually years. Tommy's grief had turned into bitterness and finally into anger. The country that he had revered and believed in had not just spat in his eye but in all of their eyes — all of those who had so little. Those who had had nothing before the War, but who had given up so much — everything sometimes — now had even less than nothing. Tommy saw it as a disgrace, and it gnawed at his very being. He accepted his own misfortune and blamed no-one for the death of Alice. That was his tragedy to bear, and he shouldered it uncomplainingly. The dearth of care for them all and the breaking of promises however, he could not bear.

Everyday his bile would rise as he would witness, on some pavement, in a shop doorway or on a corner, an old sweat sat with his medals pinned proudly across his chest. Wherever he went he would always find one. Inevitably they would have a tin mug pushed in front of them, or perhaps it was a small suitcase, or their upturned cap. They may have created a small placard that would be hanging around their neck or bent in half so that it stood on the ground by the mug, or case, or hat. The sign would be asking for some charity, a helping hand out of the gutter that they had found themselves in. Some asked for a penny or two, others pleaded for a job, a route back to their dignity. These men were inevitably silent, their eyes cast down to the floor, their shoulders rounded, concaving their chests. Tommy could feel their shame, their desperate urge for the earth to swallow them and release them from the purgatory in which they existed. To Tommy their silence was a spectacle that shouted out to him, loudly and aggressively. He felt useless in their presence as he had nothing that he could offer them, all he could do was pity them and be thankful that he wasn't yet amongst them. Many of these desperate men would be missing limbs, vacant trouser legs or flapping sleeves indicating the sacrifices that they had made. Others had wounds that weren't so easily concealed. Children would baulk and cry at them. They weren't victims, beggars, the destitute or any other pitiful name that was so freely expounded. Those with their wounds naked to the world were monsters that should be hidden from the innocent. No one should have to witness the man who has half his jaw missing, or whose face has melted down his head, or whose gaping hole in the middle of his face signifies where his nose once was. To many in the outside world who had not tasted the harsh rigours of war, they were considered monsters to be shied away from.

Limbless or faceless, Tommy saw them all as individuals who had walked in similar shoes to himself, and they in particular were the evidence of how much his country cared about them all, and of how much a land fit for heroes Britain had become.

He would never stop to talk; he couldn't bear to think that they would think him patronising. But his heart ached within him.

Once, he noticed a commotion further down the street along which he was walking. One voice raised and angry, bellowing down to a shape beneath him. As he walked the scene grew bigger, the voice more audible.

'Get yourself a job you lazy bastard.'

The words were spat out and were accompanied by a raised foot kicking down into a shape on the ground. Tommy automatically increased his speed, lengthening his stride.

'Come on, get up, what's wrong with you, you're ok, have some pride, have some dignity, you're nothing but a disgrace to us all.'

More prods into the shape which was forming into the figure of a lad sat upright, motionless apart from the inevitable reaction to the blows.

Tommy began to run. An arm was raised that held a stick of some description. He ran faster. The arm dropped, the weapon striking the shoulder of the seated man. It rocked him, but he made no other reaction. The arm raised again, readying itself for another attempt.

Tommy stretched with his stride and his arms. He thrust out with his hand and grabbed the assailants falling arm before it was able to connect with its victim again.

Tommy had made few assumptions as he raced to the scene. He had perceived an unfairness, little else, but he was surprised when he grabbed the raised arm to find that it was much thinner than he was expecting, even covered with a thick overcoat, his fingers could tell there was little flesh covering the bones. The arm gave in easily and quickly to his grasp and automatically the body spun towards him.

In surprise Tommy released his grip and stepped back. He was confused and felt that he must have misjudged the scene. He looked at the form on the floor, then back at the attacker. Then did it again. His head spun with confusion.

'He's a bastard, a lazy bastard, that's what he is, a bastard.' The voice of the stick wielder screamed.

Tommy wondered for a second if he had interfered with some domestic dispute.

'A lazy bastard,' the arm came up again, and Tommy automatically grabbed it again, but gently, just strongly enough to stop it from carrying out its intentions.

'My Billy wouldn't ever have given in like him, look at him, lazy bastard. My Billy would be working. He would have been doing something with his life. Not like this useless shit.' Spit suddenly sailed out of the mouth in a massive glob and landed on the chest of the figure who had yet to say a word or show any sense of acknowledgement of what was going on.

'Look at him, two arms, two legs, he ain't got nothing missing. You're a lazy bastard wanting the rest of the world to look after you. Get yourself a job.' The voice screamed again.

Tommy was keenly aware that he was struck dumb, he was searching for words to calm or control the situation, but he was failing. On the floor, barely having moved, with his medals pinned against his chest and a scarf stretched in front of him with a few pennies thrown onto it was one of those veterans that Tommy was so familiar with. It was true that he didn't have any obvious missing parts, but everything about him otherwise portrayed him as having served his country.

In Tommy's right hand was the wizened arm of a woman.

Her eyes were aflame, and her mouth was the filthiest he had ever experienced from a woman, let alone one so advanced in years.

'Bastard, fucking bastard.' She screamed again and tried to kick the lad.

Tommy pulled her back, 'What's going on here? Has he done something to you?' he managed to get out, feeling almost as if he were taking the role of a policeman. How he wished a bobby would suddenly turn up.

'No, he hasn't done anything to me, look he's just a lazy bastard, my Billy would never have given in like him. My Billy was a fighter.'

Tommy looked from the woman to the focus of her attention. He was still silent, but his head had raised slightly and now he was looking at both of them. Still there were no obvious markings of conflict, but in his eyes, Tommy saw the dark emptiness that he saw in so many eyes, sometimes even in his own. They were the pools of the hopeless.

He turned back to the old woman.

'Was Billy your son ma'am? Your husband?'

For the first time she looked at Tommy. Her eyes were watery and grey with the shadow of cataracts appearing on both. He felt the resistance in her arm disappear and suddenly she was merely a bag of bones held loosely together.

'He wouldn't have given in,' she muttered, softly now in a broken voice.

Tommy looked down at the lad. His head was bowed again as if everything that was going on around him was of no relevance, that he wasn't even aware of the anger he had inadvertently caused by his presence.

'He would never have given in,' she repeated, her head lowering as tears began to stream down her cheeks.

'Never,' she said even quieter.

'Can I take you home?' Tommy asked. She looked up at him, confused and lost.

'Yes please,' she answered. 'Nightingale Street.'

Tommy took her hand gently in his and wheeled her away. He looked back at the figure. 'Sorry mate, I'll be back,' he said but there was no response. If the body held any soul or consciousness, it was hidden deeply.

Tommy understood the hole that the lad was in, it was the same despair that he himself felt every day. Most of them felt it, but most managed to cope in one form or another. That poor bastard had succumbed totally to it and all his hope had disappeared.

For Tommy it was the boredom that ground his will down. Grief he had come to terms with and though he would never see his Alice again, she was with him every morning when he awoke and every evening when he fell asleep. But the boredom, the mundanity of his days was sapping his very will to survive. Every day the same. Long, lonely and often hopeless. A hot brew and a slice of toast for breakfast and then out the front door. Pounding streets, knocking on doors, offering his services to help with the gardening or cleaning the windows or perhaps some decorating. Anything that needed doing he could do, and for just a few small pennies.

Some days he would line up with hundreds of other hopefuls at the factory gates, praying that today would be his lucky day, today he would take home a pay packet. And sometimes it was his lucky day, sometimes, but not often. The finger would point at him, or his shoulder would be grabbed, and he would be thrust through the gates. Most days however he would leave with all the others, reduced slightly, a little smaller than the man that had woken up in his bed that morning.

Tommy had felt the ache of boredom before. The days in the trenches had been filled with it, unending minutes that had to be survived. It hadn't all been fun and games, excitement packed days of killing the Boche! In reality he had probably only fired his rifle in anger half a dozen or so times.

He had been on the Somme of course, at Loos, Arras, Passchendaele, all in the thick of it, and there were a couple, a few perhaps, other occasions that he had had cause to pull that trigger on his Lee Enfield. But in all his time, almost four years, there had been very little excitement and an awful amount of boredom. Nevertheless, Tommy, like all of the lads, found ways to fill his time. Inevitably it would start as soon as they had stood down off their fire-steps each morning — with the Germans failing to materialise in their attacking hoards. Breakfast would be laboured over; every detail of the meal being prolonged as far as was possible. And then it would become an exercise in creativity, sometimes under orders, usually not. Habitually Tommy would spend as much time as he could cleaning his rifle, polishing away every last sign of dirt and ensuring that it was in the best working condition possible. Then he might darn his socks or mend some sandbags, write letters home, play some cards, find new ways to reduce the rat population, and perhaps the most satisfying task, albeit usually for just a few minutes relief — popping lice. He would take a lit candle and run the flame as close to the seams of his tunic to try and burn as much of the infestation as he could. Rarely did it give him much respite from their irritations, but the satisfaction of hearing the eggs and their little bodies explode filled him with a rare positivity in the trenches.

They all did it. They found ways of making minutes and

hours move just a little bit faster, and they did it together, for each other. They were all in the same situation, knowing that they had to survive time as much as anything and they knew they needed to do it as a unit. So, they did. They would make light of their situation, they would play jokes on each other, sing songs together, share their dirty French postcards around. One way or another they had to get to the end of each day, and one way or another they knew that they wouldn't be doing it forever, they wouldn't always be in a trench. And so, they could bear it. They could manage the boredom because there was a purpose to it.

Now though, thought Tommy, what was the purpose of his boredom? How did he know where it would end? If it would ever end? Where was the light at the end of the tunnel? He had no idea. And this boredom was engulfed in loneliness. There was none of the camaraderie they had felt in the trenches. Every day and all day, he was alone and looking after himself on his own. Even when he was at the factory gates with hundreds of others like him, he was alone — he could only care about his own success, his own chance of a job for a day, his own survival. His life had become one of total insularity.

And the hunger that he felt! It was unforgiving. Every morning he would wake up and it was as if his stomach was digesting itself, gnawing away at his insides. He hadn't starved in the trenches, hardly even ever felt hunger. Far from it. He reckoned he had been about a stone heavier when he came out of the lines than he had been in 1914, a good two stone heavier than he now weighed. Of course, the food hadn't been the greatest ever produced, and admittedly the rations were smaller in the latter years than they had been at the beginning, but bully beef and biscuits, Tickler's marmalade and toast, and Maconochie's stew all sustained them. Even when the rations felt meagre and unpalatable, there was plenty of food sent from home and it all got shared around. Sometimes there were so many cakes being sent up the lines that they almost became part of the trench system, squeezed into gaps in the sandbag walls. In the direst of circumstances and the darkest of days, they rarely went hungry.

Tommy's stomach spasmed as if it could read his mind and he began to think about the best meals that he could ever remember. They would always be had on the coldest of nights. The middle of winter. Freezing nights that had been pre-empted by drawn out days of unforgiving cold. All day they would concentrate on merely staying as warm as possible. Keeping frostbite from the extremities. Huddling together for support and shared warmth.

Then eventually, a little after dusk, word would get round that food was on the way. In a Pavlovian reaction to the memory Tommy's mouth watered slightly. He remembered the whole emotion of receiving the news, on those nights. The relief and anticipation that he would feel knowing that hot Maconochie's stew was imminent.

It didn't matter that the meat was mainly fat and gristle, it was having something warm in his stomach that would make his mouth water. The fun would start with the desperate search for the location of the food. The lads together would look for the signs, then once someone had spotted them, it would be shared like a bag of sweets. A chimney of steam wisping up into the darkening sky, invisible to the untrained eye, was the clue. Along with the rest, Tommy would follow its journey, unbearably slow on its way towards them. And as the journey progressed that chimney of steam would get a little lower in the sky, making it increasingly difficult to judge its whereabouts. But then, eventually there they would be, with a vat, standing before him, the bringers of warmth and sustenance. Tommy would hold out his bowl and they would ladle the oily, vaguely nutritional liquid into it. He would back away, sit himself down on an unused part of the firestep, or move into a dugout, his spoon at the ready, polished to a dull sheen. He would skim the spoon over the surface of the stew in order to prolong and savour the meal for as long as was possible. He would bring the spoon to his lips, preparing himself for the warm nectar that he had craved. It would arrive, drip onto his tongue, the anticipation was gone. But time and again the stew would fail to live up to its expectation, rather than relieving the cold in his body for a moment it would inevitably add to it. The chill air through which it had passed on its long and arduous journey through the lines had reduced the heat to nothing. But all the lads had learnt to deal with and accommodate every circumstance, and Tommy was well versed in coping with a cold dinner.

Every time he lived in hope, but when disappointed by the cold liquid, he would do what they all did, dig deeply into his pack for his small tin container of pepper. Then opening it slowly to avoid spilling any of the precious contents, he would pour it liberally onto his awaiting food. Then, once again he would take his spoon over the stew, raise it to his lips and sample it. This time it would indeed be the food of the gods. The pepper made it burning hot. From his toes, to his knees, to his shivering belly he was infused with heat and the rest of the stew wouldn't be gracefully supped but downed in as short a number of greedy gulps as was possible.

Those meals, taken on cold winter's nights at the end of cold winter's days, were the best meals he had ever experienced in his life. Perhaps it was the momentary relief from the chill that they brought that gave them such strength. Perhaps it was the fact that after the first signal that food was on the way, he would have to wait in anticipation for the meal to arrive which lent it a supernatural power. Whatever it was, it was a culinary delight which far surpassed the summer rations. And in comparison, to what his meals were now, it was truly ambrosia.

The bitterness of hunger and ennuie gnawed at Tommy's very essence as he recalled that cold winter's stew. He deserved more. They all deserved more. After all that he had given his country — years of his life in service. He deserved more. Yes, he had been one of the lucky ones. Yes, he had got to the end. And no, he didn't take the loss of his wonderful Alice personally — it wasn't God's punishment to him for wrongs committed. It was just fate. It's what happened. It's what he had seen so many times throughout his life. From a celestial roll of the dice a shard of shrapnel could travel twenty yards and snag your jugular vein, or it could miss you by an inch and puncture a sandbag; or an outbreak of cholera could attack a whole community and kill all with the exception of an aging widow. It was all just chance. Nothing personal. What he couldn't accept was the misery brought upon not by fate but by social inequality and decision making by the very ones that had made promises to them all. It was this misery that embittered him. With every passing of a stranger with medals and a placard, his bile would rise and the disgust he felt for the country would be compounded. A country fit for heroes? It was a joke to him, a wicked, tasteless joke. The country was a disgrace. He had sincerely believed that having fought, lived, eaten and suffered amongst all manner of men, that the country they returned to would have a greater evenness spread over it. He had physically pulled toffs from the mud of Flanders, shared food with bankers and teachers and accountants, gone over the top with labourers and factory workers and boys half his age. They were all the same, just blokes, none of them special. He had had no real prejudices against anyone, he saw men as men, none better, few worse. Whether their bank accounts were overflowing, or they had lived on a hand-to-mouth existence he hadn't judged them, they were all born into this world the same way, where they had fallen was pure chance; nothing else. Those that whined about inequality and the privilege of toffs he ignored, theirs were the words of life's failures, those that refused to take responsibility of their own lives, that couldn't accept luck, good or bad, for what it was, a random, ungoverned force of nature. He knew instinctively that any man with nothing in his pocket would swap places with the man with everything if he could, and therefore, why should he deign to moan about those with more than he? Tommy had been born into a frugal and simple life with few material privileges, but with the love of his mother he had never wanted for anything. All his life since he had felt the comfort of his mother's love or that love of his dear Alice, he had never been poor, hard done by or underprivileged.

But now, he had become embittered by the scant regard the country, his country, gave to him and to all of those that he had stood side by side with. A great empire, the proudest nation on the seas, the land of Shakespeare and Dickens, Stevenson, Brunel, Darwin, Newton and Nelson! And how did it treat those of its own, who suffered, often through no fault of their own? What did it give those who had risked all and often gave everything for the country's agendas? Nothing! That's what the country gave them. Nothing. It was this that embittered Tommy. He looked beyond his own self, his own ability to make the best of his life and looked at those who didn't possess his gifts of self-belief and tenacity and capability. He saw their hopelessness and his heart broke for them and his soul turned sour against the country.

Tommy knew that he could and would survive. Not because of any hospitality, care or humanity issued to him by the nation, but because he was strong both in mind and limb. He would get up every day, make himself a brew and then go out looking for work, any work, that would sustain him through another day or two. He would get up for as long as he physically could, and he would not be defeated by life. But he would do it in the full knowledge that he was alone in his world and the promises that had been given to them were forgotten and sterile. A land fit for heroes? It was a joke. Britain was a sick canker on the earth and the evidence was in every town for all to see.

PART 3
TYNE COT CEMETERY
November 1927

Tommy gripped the rake handle firmly as he worked. He had never taken more pride in his work than he did now — no leaf was permitted to rest anywhere on the hallowed turf that he considered his own personal responsibility. As he paced slowly between the Portland stone markers, his eyes searched endlessly for any fault in the garden, any blemish that he could eradicate to keep the carpet pristine.

It was late in the season for falling leaves, but they still did find their way in, and he as a custodian, would not allow any to remain for long. This job had become his life, his purpose, his sanity.

The epiphany had come suddenly one crisp morning when the thought of stepping out of his bed into the chill air had delayed the start to his day. He was a child again, just for a moment, and wanted to hug his blankets to him, to sink deeply into the thin mattress and cover his head with the pillow. He could almost hear his mother's voice calling him, ordering him out of bed and to the kitchen sink for that thirty second, ice cold wash that would both wake him and torture him, he could almost smell the fatty bacon in his mother's frying pan. Tasting his childhood again he was momentarily not the bitter, middle-aged man that he had become. For a few scant breaths he was that boy that he had been, with dreams and beliefs. He was an optimist and blissfully naive and this boy whispered to him, almost like a spectre from a grave, his own grave. It whispered to him the perfect wisdom of the young, the dying, and the contented. It whispered that today was a new day. Today was the only day that mattered. Today was the perfect day. The ghost of his youth spoke kindly but sternly and told him that the time had now come to move on, his bitterness must be put to rest and he must once again take responsibility of his life, his present and his future.

As the voice spoke to him the anger and pain and bitterness began slowly to dissolve from his mind. The shouting that reverberated constantly through his head, a screaming of anger at the world, quietened, slowed and became distant.

Cajoled by the voice of his past he slid out from the bedclothes, then guided by an unseen hand he dressed, washed, and had his brew and two thin slices of toast with the last remnants of a slab of butter spread thinly over. An observer might assume that Tommy had sunk into a mindless insanity, as he appeared to be speaking to another, in truth he was speaking simply to himself. The self of another time and the self of that day. His eyes had been dulled by life, but a barely perceptible sparkle was beginning to glisten just on the edges of his pupils. Life was returning to his eyes as it had tried so many times before, but this morning Tommy was allowing it.

He sought out a barely functional canvas cloth bag and stuffed it with clothes, washing utensils, a mug, plate, bowl, knife, fork, spoon, his bible, and the only photo that he had of dear Alice. He emptied a tobacco tin of the few shillings and pence that he had managed to accrue beyond his living costs and stuffed them deep into his jacket pocket. It didn't matter that the money was so little, that it could barely cover a few meals, he had been used to living off scraps, making pennies last longer than most would imagine and enduring a rugged life that cost nothing but physical inconvenience.

He glanced round the simple home for anything else that might prove useful and decided on including a couple of pencils, paper and an old copy of *The Return of Sherlock Holmes*. Then he turned his back on whatever remained and walked to the front door. Turning the key in the lock and then lifting the catch he felt nothing more than purpose in his actions. He pulled the door to him and stepped out into the world. The door swung closed, he turned and locked it. Then put the key deeply into his bag. And he walked away.

The weather was kind to him. It was cold but dry and the road melted beneath his steps. He was marching once again like he had done so many times during his service careers and though he marched alone he felt the presence of others with him. He marched with their voices singing in his head — marching songs that helped to eat up the miles with their patriotic fervour or comic vulgarity. As he marched, he felt less alone than he had done since the day he returned and found his Alice gone and rather than tire with his exertions it was as if each hour on the road gave him renewed energy and vigour, more purpose and more belief in what he was doing and where he was going. When night fell, he found a wall to huddle against and rested. The *keevit* of a hunting tawny owl brought him comfort and he slept, not for long, but soundly. Before the sun was up Tommy was setting forth with a ration of bread and cheese in his stomach and a goal in his mind.

Sometime before midday a lorry slowed by him and stopped. The driver offered a lift and Tommy gratefully accepted. He was younger than Tommy but not by much and his face bore the familiar weathered signs of wartime experiences. In each other they saw a familiarity and a solidarity and though they spoke little in their journey, they said plenty. By nightfall they were at the coast and wishing each other well. With the sound of the waves, the smell of the salt and the calls of the gulls, Tommy felt that he was further from his home and closer to his goal than he actually was. His destination felt so tantalisingly near that impatience gripped him and sleeping that night, on the quay, was harder than it had been against the previous night's stone wall.

He knew that the money in his pocket wouldn't buy him a fare across the Channel, but he believed and hoped that he could successfully convince a captain to accept an offering, or barter a ticket for his labour. He needed neither. His appearance was neither that of a vagrant or a scrounger, despite his years away from the forces his demeanour was still that of a man who knew the responsibility of the khaki and to anyone with similar experiences he shone like a beacon. It was the Quay Master that identified his cause first and he approached Tommy with an affection and seriousness that belied his otherwise gruff nature.

'You're wanting to go back ain't ya?' he stated rather than asked. 'Back to see the boys?'

'I suppose so,' admitted Tommy. 'I feel it pulling like a magnet. Not just the lads, but the whole place.'

'Ave you got a ticket? An offer of transport?'

'No. Not yet. But I will.'

'Come with me lad.' The Quay Master turned with full expectation that he would be obeyed.

'Lad!' Tommy thought. 'I'm still a lad, that's how he sees me. With my coarse complexion, greyed hair and ageing gait, nothing has changed. We were all lads back then, all of us, regardless of vintage, and we are all lads now, and we shall remain lads until the day we die. To each other anyhow. That's just the way it is.'

Tommy unquestioningly pulled himself to his feet and followed the man into the quay and towards a jetty. Life was everywhere. Fishermen were loading their boats, calling to each other with advice and information on the weather forecast. Others were completing maintenance to their vessels or their nets and pots. The fishing season in all reality was in its last days of the year but the men were still aiming to eke out a little more from the seas.

'Jack, Jack Cavendish. I've got a passenger for you,' the Quay Master called down into one of the smallest boats bobbing in the uneasy waters. A face appeared from below decks with tousled hair and an unkempt beard.

'I don't take passengers, you know that,' the face stated.

'And I don't ever check your boat properly when you come into dock Jack, but this time you will take a passenger, or I will be doing a good and thorough search of every nook and cranny in that barrel of yours when you get back in — regardless of the time or the lashing of the rain. He's one of us Jack, one of the lads, now do something right and drop him near the port, he can sort himself from there.'

Jack grumbled something into the forest of hairs around his mouth, beckoned Tommy down onto the deck and turned back into the depths of his boat.

The crossing was pleasant enough. Tommy had had no clearly defined plan of how he would cross the Channel, he had just hoped on providence, and providence had indeed come to his aid. Jack's boat was small and cramped and clearly, he was unused to taking passengers with him. But he was hospitable enough and shared his coffee and sandwiches willingly and generously. It was clear to Tommy that the nets and lobster pots were all for show on the boat, Jack had no intention of dropping them overboard at any time and they remained in place and untroubled when they eventually sailed into a small cove close to the Calais beaches. It was after dusk and the waters were dark but calm. Tommy helped the boatman ease a small dinghy into the water and they both climbed in and rowed quietly to the land.

'Here you go fella, head up the bank there and you'll find the Calais road. Safe travels and good luck.' Jack shook Tommy's hand and offered him half of the malt loaf that was his provision for the return journey.

Tommy hadn't been inquisitive over the sailor's mission. He had assumed, somewhere in the recesses of his mind that Jack traded in wine from the continent, but he hadn't sought to prove his theory and certainly wouldn't consider questioning Jack about it. Jack's business was of no business to himself and he wouldn't disrespect the kindness of his host by prying.

He left with a simple word of thanks and headed in the direction that he had been advised. The air was already too cold for comfort and he felt that he ought to find some sort of shelter as soon as possible, though whether any of his English shillings would be of any use he had no idea.

It was an easy climb from the cove with the path leading straight onto a road and in the near distance he could see the lit windows of buildings which he hoped were inns or pensions. For two nights he had been quite happy, prepared even to suffer the night's chill, it had felt like part of the experience, part of the mental journey as well as the physical one. His great coat had been the same comforter as it had been on so many previous occasions. A shield to the air and a protection against the hardness of an unmattressed ground. Now though Tommy had a sudden urge for company within solid walls.

In England his existence had been one of solitude and

independence since the moment he had stepped back through his front door in returning from the Western Front. His shield to the grief of losing Alice and the disinterest of a country to his returning generation was his own insularity. Living alone, working in his own cocoon, he was protected, and this protection had enabled him to take each long minute one at a time and survive it. Now, from the moment that he stepped onto the French beach he had felt that mantle of protection, fall away. He felt his solitude and a loneliness came over him like a fog. He yearned for company. In France he felt instantly as if he had returned home. Not home in the sense of a land or physical building, but in the sense of community. This was where he had left his soul and his other family with whom he had shared so many experiences and traumas. Some of them had joined him on the boat back to Shorncliffe in Kent, others had left him weeks, months and years previously. Yet they were all family. They were all connections. And now he felt their absence keenly.

In England the Front had been something to forget, to bury deeply into the trenches of his mind never to be exhumed. The faces, the voices, the noise, smell, sights suddenly were back and welcoming him on the French soil. They wrapped around him and embraced him.

The lights in the distance beckoned to him and he marched towards them, hoping that a hospitality of some description would be offered.

The first lit buildings were houses, homes emanating private lives, but a short distance further on there was a typical auberge. These lights were bright, and the door swung frequently from those entering and leaving.

Tommy entered and half a dozen pairs of eyes turned from their companions to enquire who the next visitor was.

'Ah! Les anglais sont revenus!' the baritone voice of a dark haired, pot-bellied giant immediately proclaimed through teeth gripping a pipe. He was clearly the owner of the inn and the tone was of undisguised joviality and welcome but the response from the patrons was of indifference and their eyes returned to their drinks, their meals and their partners.

Tommy strode towards the giant, who proffered a small table and chair. 'Bienvenu Anglais! Que désirez-vous?'

Tommy sat down and delved into his pocket for the English money, pulled it out and threw it onto the table.

'Qu'est-ce que c'est? Argent anglais? C'est pas bien!' The inn keeper pushed the money back towards Tommy with a frown, looking directly into his eyes and shook his head. Then he smiled. 'Attendez mon ami,' he said and turned and walked back towards his bar.

A few minutes passed then the landlord returned with a tray bearing a carafe of wine and a glass, a plate with cheese, an apple and a long French stick. 'Avec mes compliments mon ami… on ze house!'

'Thank you,' Tommy replied. 'It's very good of you, très bon, très gentil.'

'Pas de tout. Enjoy!'

Tommy tucked in gratefully. As he sat there and ate he felt as if tension was lifting that had been plaguing him for what seemed like an eternity. The inn was warm both in heat and ambience and the quiet banter of the French locals washed the walls with a hospitality that Tommy had shunned back in England. France wasn't his home, Calais had little to do with his war, but here he felt a relaxation of the bitterness that had afflicted him in the country that he sincerely felt had failed him and all those like him. In England he had felt alone, not just because of the failures of the government but by his own insistence to retreat into his shell and push the everyday goodwill of his neighbours away. There they didn't understand the experiences of the lads, only the lads understood it, the lads that had experienced that existence. In England the returning were welcomed with open arms and tears of joy and then with expectations that life would go back to normal, old skills and employments would be taken up again without a backward thought, "thank God, you're home, now you can go back into the factory, the farm, the mine, the school, the bank or the shop."

In France everyone had experienced what the lads had experienced. Even here at the coast which had been saved by direct conflict the soil seemed to speak of the abuse that it had suffered a few short miles inland, the trees whispered of the annihilation of their brethren just down the road and the buildings perhaps wept for all those that had been smashed into unrecognisable rubble. Every citizen walking the streets, sleeping in beds and drinking in ale houses knew of the war. The young, the old, the men, the women, the children all felt it keenly. It was a knowledge not read about in newspapers or periodicals; it was a knowledge acquired through the hands-on touch of the war. Here the country knew what it was to be a veteran. Knew, understood and empathised and silently it shook Tommy's hand and bid him welcome, sit down, rest and ease your mind, your experiences are shared here.

Tommy ate and drank and felt his heart return. In this inn he didn't feel like a stranger or a foreigner. And as he sat, he felt the heat of a tear in the corner of his eye, and then its slow, coursing passage down his cheekbone to the side of his chin. He felt it and allowed it to complete its journey. Then another came, and another and soon Tommy's face was awash with the releasing of his pain. Silently and without motion, he wept. If any of the patrons noticed his tears, they didn't show it, they allowed him his space, his time, his release. The landlord saw and smiled sadly. He cleared the plate of food and refilled the wine glass then placed his big hand upon Tommy's shoulder and spoke quietly, gently into his ear.

'Restez ici, Monsieur. Stay. You are welcome. You are of many, beaucoup, beaucoup. Stay. Rest. Vous vous retrouverez.'

And Tommy did stay. He stayed until the carafe was empty and his eyes were dry. He stayed until he was the lone customer and the embers of the fire were glowing for their final time. Then unintentionally, he fell asleep. His arms crossed in front of him on the table and his head resting on the back of his chair. The landlord covered him with a blanket, left a solitary candle burning on the fireplace hearth and went to bed.

When he awoke it was well past dawn, sometime in the mid-morning. There were the sounds of life outside the inn, bicycles squeaking by, chatter, gulls, the occasional neighing of a horse. The inn was dark with the window shutters blocking most of the daylight, but it was light enough for Tommy to remember where he was. Suddenly he needed to empty his bladder and he felt an odd panic grip him with the knowledge that he had no idea where he could do so without embarrassment. He stumbled through the small inn, knocking into chairs and tables which were invisible in the half-light then found by courtesy of luck, a back door. It was latched, but not locked and he pulled it open. The shock of the cold air only exasperated the pain in his groin, but he stepped out and saw that he was in a small courtyard with the very obvious stable door of a latrine in front of him.

As he stood pissing into the small, stinking hole in the ground he watched the dark yellow stream leave his body, burning his prick as it did so, and he saw there and then the last vestiges of his pain and anger leaving him.

Before he left the inn, he searched for something that he could leave for his host. A token of his appreciation and a sign of his comprehension of what he had been given. All he felt that he had suitable to give was his bible. He opened it and inside the front cover he wrote with his pencil, 'Merci, Merci, Merci'.

Two days later he was back. Back where it had all happened. Back from where they had wanted so much to escape. Where they had all grown so old in such a short space of time. Where they had experienced a life that they had never imagined.

Ypres was practically unrecognisable from the town that he had left less than nine years before. Then the town had been a wasteland of rubble and destruction where he could have sat on a horse in the middle of the square and been able to see from one side of the town to the other, such was the devastation. But now, in walking in through the Lille Gate the town was far from being ruinous. Certainly, there was still plenty of evidence of the years of conflict, but there was a greater impression of rebirth. It was as if he was returning on the ninth year of gestation, that the town was preparing to burst once more from its protective womb and become again the hub of Europe that it had once been. Tommy wandered around with little aim other than to remember, to gather his thoughts, to make sense of it all. He was led by the ghosts of his past who had no interest in time or distance, just a desire for Tommy to see everything. As he walked and breathed in the air of a town that had at one time been the entrance to hell, he didn't feel the hatred and fear that he might have expected, he didn't feel the renewing of past tensions. He felt a calm. He felt that he was home.

Whereas in England his own existence appeared to him to be

soulless and the lives of others pointless and banal, here by the Cloth Hall he felt the community of communal effort. The air was filled with noise. The noise of humans being human, being normal. People calling to each other, talking and shouting at one another. Voices in a multitude of dialects and accents. Mixed within the French and Flemish there was just as much English and even some German. The town had not forgotten its war, it couldn't. The evidence was everywhere, but it wasn't wasting away from the bitterness of the years it had had to endure. Instead, Ypres was like the flower pushing through the rubble to find the sun. The Cloth Hall was no longer the few small, dilapidated walls that he had known, now it was a tall, powerful, statement of a building that dominated its surroundings, reminding all that passed it of its glorious history as the economic focal point of Western Europe. A hundred yards or so from the Cloth Hall, the equally imposing Menin Gate, newly opened, beckoned Tommy to it. When he and so many others had marched from Ypres to the Front along the Menin Road, they had done so through a gate in name only, a break in the ramparts of the medieval fortifications and a crossing of the moat. Now the gate stood huge on the skyline, offering comfort and security to those within the walls of the town, and threat and defiance to those wishing to attack it. He walked towards the gate and as he neared it his steps slowed, he was transfixed by the stature of the construction, awe overwhelming him, emotion washing over his mind. This was more than a gate, more than a defence against future violence. It was a magnificent memorial to all of those that had passed through, many never to return. Tommy strode slowly but purposely through its arches, around its walls and then back again to walk from West to East. He gazed up at the all-powerful lions sitting there proudly, challenging, daring any enemy to try to take the town. Then he leant on the wall of the bridge covering the moat and covered his eyes. Here in Ypres, they were all remembered. Here they weren't cast aside. Here they lived, all of them, for all eternity — not just those that were lost to the mortal earth, but those still that existed but as ghosts. The names of the lost were all painstakingly chipped into the walls and arches, those that had fallen, never to be found in the Salient were the epitaph for all of them. Those that had returned and those that had not. They were there, side by side with their comrades, even if their names were waiting to be carved on a different stone in a different town in years to come. This was the memorial to all of them.

Tommy had never seen anything like the Menin Gate, he had never believed that his country would care as much to create something so monumental. The irony of how Britain had looked after its dead better than it did its living flitted over his mind, but to him the Gate was an understanding. It was a nod to them all. Maybe not an apology, but certainly the proclamation that they would not be forgotten — any of them.

Tommy was exhausted, more from the shedding of the bitterness that he had carried for so long than from his journeying. He climbed back towards the top of the memorial and took the path along the ramparts, it was the ending of summer and though still warm the light was fading, but he meant to feel every minute. There was a sense of peace on the walk, small trees that had only been planted in the recent past gave an almost park-like quality to the mound. The occasional squirrel, blackbird, robin or jackdaw enhanced the feeling of nature returning to reclaim a part of its treasured land. A black Labrador bound past him chasing a stick, then its owner turned, smiled and greeted him with a welcome as he too passed Tommy. Tommy's steps were slow but not laboured, he was soaking up the atmosphere, bathing in the peace of mind that it was giving him, he was perhaps even sauntering.

Soon he was at an iron gate in a small, new, red brick wall. Over the wall were lines of headstones, not many — perhaps two hundred of them, maybe fewer, all facing towards the water of the moat of the town. As he looked over the wall it was like looking into someone's private domain, he felt that to enter would be an intrusion, even just peering in was an invasion of privacy. The pure white of the headstones stood within a well kempt lawn with trees, bushes and flowers all around. This was a garden that he was looking into. Not a cemetery or graveyard of the dead, but a garden of the sleeping. Within it he almost felt that the birds were singing louder, more joyfully, more freely.

Quietly, as if not to awaken or disturb the residents, he lifted the simple latch and pushed the gate open. It squeaked as he did so, as all gates do, and he cursed quietly at himself for his thoughtlessness. Then he stepped softly inside and gently eased the gate closed behind him.

To Tommy's left stood proudly and erect the Sword of Sacrifice, in front of him the men rested. The white of the Portland Stone shone in the afternoon light and seemed to underline that this wasn't a place of gloom or depression but of solace and hope and peace. The men that were in front of him seemed present in every way, resting but not gone. He walked softly amongst them, reading the occasional name, rank, regiment, age and the occasional inscription. Knowing them, meeting them. Musselwhite from the Royal Irish Rifles. Neason aged 21, a New Zealand engineer. Captain Anderson of the Royal Fusiliers. Burbidge of the Wiltshires. Ockelford whose inscription stopped Tommy in his tracks, *Gone but not forgotten from his loving wife and baby Peggy.* A simple inscription that brought Ockelford and his family right to the surface of the lawn, put skin and clothes on his bones, put his wife and baby Peggy right there at his side, leaning over the stone, crying silently, dignified, devastated but not broken. At three pence a letter that inscription had cost his wife dearly, too dearly for the widow of a thirty-year-old lance corporal in the Royal Engineers, so dearly that she couldn't afford to place her own name alongside her daughter's, so she chose to immortalise her child. April 21, 1918, he died. The great German Offensive that brought everyone out to the front lines to repel them. The massive push that almost won the war for the Germans before the sheer weight of numbers of the Americans could sway the balance inexorably in favour of the Allies. The push did get stopped, just outside Ypres and the war got turned, but it killed Ockelford, and baby Peggy would grow up without knowing her father.

Tommy turned from the stone and looked down at the green, but still waters of the moat. Two Great Crested Grebes glided past, their heads held high before suddenly disappearing along with the rest of their bodies as they dove like arrows into the depths. Tommy sat down onto his haunches, and then onto his backside. He placed his bag carefully to his side and pulled his knees up to his chest, wrapping his arms around them. He looked into the water, into the depths, the translucence and the mists which swam there. He dove further into the fog, deeper and deeper as his mind groped outwardly for the images of the past, seeking the sights that had been so familiar and trying now to put them back in place. In place of where he had arrived. He pursued Ypres, "Wipers", of old. The dereliction, destruction, chaos. The trenches filled with water and rats and louse infestation and stinking bodies and terror and boredom and friendship. He searched for the shell holes that were sanctuary in an offensive, the clatter and rattle of Maxim Guns and the great pounding blasts of the five nines, the spirals of barbed wire and the blood and bone shards on his tunic that didn't belong to himself. He pursued the eyes of the men that he had killed, the enemy that he had seen dying and not helped, the friends or non-enemies that had been broken into tiny fragments of themselves. He delved deeper and deeper, every ounce of memory tested for clarification and verification. Every sense quizzed for a remembrance. The weedy tentacles of death brushed by his diving mind as he sought the stones and gravel of his memory's floor. He found it all there in his head, not stagnant and festering like some poisoned pool of filth as he had let it be for so long, but a sediment filled tide filtering through the crevices of his consciousness. His mind swam further along that bed and the memories became less dark, less unfiltered, clearer, real and eventually just memories, no longer nightmares. His mind pushed upwards to the light of the day.

In his reverie Tommy had been oblivious to the opening of the gate or the soft trudge of footsteps towards him. He hadn't sensed the presence of another's breath behind him, but with the touch upon his shoulder he was propelled back beside Lance Corporal Ockelford.

'You ok fella?' It was a voice of compassion and understanding.

Tommy turned sharply round, but his mind was still fogged by his thoughts. 'Fine, I'm fine, thank you, just thinking,' he replied.

'Beautiful, isn't it? Here. By the waters. It's where I would want to be.'

He was wearing a dark wool suit and had a bushy handle-bar

moustache that fell just below his lower lip, his eyes were slightly watery and angled down, creases covered his forehead and cheeks. In years he was younger than he looked but the age of his life defined his face.

Tommy's response was barely more than a grunt of agreement.

'First time back, is it?' the man questioned as he lowered himself down to the ground to sit next to Tommy. 'A lot come back you know,' he continued without waiting for a response from Tommy. 'It's like a calling. They have to come back to put it behind them. To get on and continue with life, with a future.'

Tommy turned and looked into the man's eyes, seeing him properly for the first time. He saw a comrade. A survivor. One that had suffered, but refused to suffer any longer. Even in repose he bore a sense of stature, but it wasn't a stature of title or superiority, more that of confidence and acceptance of his role in life and in the world in general.

'I never left you know, couldn't bear it really, leaving here. Had nothing to return home to, all my folks were dead, I'd never married. It was just me. And somehow at the end, when it all stopped, went quiet, I couldn't see anywhere to be but here. With the lads. It was the only place that I felt I could have a purpose. Trying to make it right, or help in some part to make it right. For all of them that weren't like me, hadn't been lucky like me, who mustn't be lost or forgotten, ever.' The man spoke in a quiet torrent of half-thoughts. It was an explanation, as if Tommy needed a reason for the man being there.

Tommy sat still, listening but not responding. Hearing and understanding but having nothing to add in reply.

'Say,' said the man. 'Are you interested in a job?' Tommy turned and looked at the man, quizzically.

'A job?' he asked.

'Yes, sure, a job. Do you want a job, or are you just passing through?'

'Yes, of course I'd like a job,' Tommy said, 'what do you have in mind?'

'Great, you can start in the morning, meet me at Hell Fire Corner at oh seven hundred. We'll take it from there. You know where Hell Fire Corner is?'

'If it's not been moved' replied Tommy. 'Is there anything I need?'

'No, I'll get you everything, but be prepared for a long day, it'll be cold at that time so wrap up warm and bring food to eat. Say, where are you staying?'

'Nowhere yet, I only just got here really. Was just finding my way around again. It's changed a lot since I was last here.'

'Right,' said the man, and he took out a pencil from his inside coat pocket and a notebook. He started scribbling in the book and then ripped out the page, proffering it to Tommy, 'here you go, get yourself to this address, it's just off the market place, you'll find it easy enough. Tell Charlotte that I sent you, that I've given you a job, and that you'll be able to pay her at the end of the week. She's a lovely lady and will make you feel welcome. Her apple pie is something to die for!'

'I don't know what to say,' said Tommy. 'Thank you, I am indebted to you, sir.'

'It's nothing my friend,' the man replied. 'We need as much help as we can get, especially now with it getting colder, you will be doing us a service. And it's a long day's work, so you will earn your wage… my name by the way is Alf, Alf Barnes. I'll see you in the morning. Have a good night.'

Alf pushed his way up from the ground and put out his hand

to Tommy. 'Tommy,' he said. 'Tommy Atkins.'

'Well, what do you know!' Alf replied. 'See you tomorrow, Tommy.' He smiled warmly and turned away.

For a moment Tommy felt a little stunned, he wasn't quite sure what had just happened. He had been back in Ypres just a few hours, on the continent a few short days, yet he had already, somehow, managed to get himself employment. He wasn't a superstitious man, or really religious, though he clung to the hope that there was perhaps something beyond the grave. But in this moment, he did feel that there was something guiding his life, almost watching over him.

In due course he got himself back up and headed out of the small cemetery and made his way back to the Cloth Hall, the focal point of the town.

It didn't take him long to find Charlotte's house. He had recognised the street name instantly as a battered sign amidst bricks and stones and slates from the days when all the lads knew all the street names by heart. Not for their value as streets, because they had been far from that, but as points of reference within the destruction. The street now was new and fresh looking but in an old, original style. Though it was clear at the moment that it hadn't been built long, Tommy mused that within a few short years, with some weathering here and there it and indeed the rest of the town, would almost look original. Original from before the war, as if it was a relic from the Middle Ages.

He rapped on the door and took a step back into the road to wait its opening. He heard voices inside, the barking of a dog, or dogs, and the quick steps of someone coming down a hallway.

Charlotte was tall and thin with short brown hair, cut almost like a boy. She was probably younger than Tommy but had that look about her that made her age hard to define. In opening the door her face immediately smiled with welcome and curiosity.

'I've been sent by Alf Barnes,' Tommy started up. 'He said that you could perhaps offer me a room? He's given me a job. I'll have money by the end of the week, I can pay you then.'

'Of course, of course, another one of Alf's men, you are welcome, come in, come in, there is plenty of room,' Charlotte replied, her accent thickly Flemish. She gave Tommy the most welcoming of smiles that he had not seen for many years, 'do you like apple pie? Belgian style? I have some just out of the oven.'

'Yes, yes, I do, thank you. My name is Atkins, Thomas Atkins.'

'Then follow me Mr Atkins, it is a pleasure to meet you. Stay for as long as you wish. You are most welcome.'

Charlotte turned back into her home, beckoning Tommy to follow and to close the door behind him. The walls of the hallway were caked with photographs and small oil paintings in ornate gold frames, a haphazard line of glass fronted cabinets filled with china and porcelain ornaments lined the corridor. Tommy inadvertently knocked into a picture and a small puff of dust rose and then fell almost back to its original perch. On the floor a succession of well-trod rugs kept the cold in check from the stone floor.

Charlotte opened a door and a terrier of some vague parentage darted out yapping noisily but wagging a tail that showed its lack of evil intentions.

'Don't worry about Frank,' she said, stretching out the vowel and implying the dog. 'He is only curious and pleased to have more visitors. Here, come in and have some pie, then I shall show you your room. If you want to eat with us later, you can, there is enough for all.'

It was an airy backroom with a small sofa and an armchair

that faced towards a fireplace that was lit and burned welcomingly. A large tabby cat sprawled in front of the flames and didn't deign to acknowledge Tommy's entrance.

'Here, sit, sit.' Charlotte insisted.

Tommy put down his bag and went to take off his overcoat.

'Ah, my mistake, I am sorry, what a host I am!' Charlotte chastised herself. 'Here, let me take your coat and your bag, you must just rest and warm yourself.' She helped Tommy off with his coat and then bent down to pick up his bag. She left the room with them and Tommy was left with his thoughts and the two animals, one of whom cared not a jot, the other who wouldn't keep its nose off Tommy's boots.

He sat down on the sofa and looked into the fire. The flames danced around, and he could feel the gentle heat emanating out towards him. The last time that he had spent a night in Ypres he probably walked up this street he mused, or rather he would have scampered up aware that it was too close to the town's boundary to be a safe haven. The shells were sent to the town by the German guns then, sporadically, not with any great intent on killing, just to torment and tease. For Tommy it was harder on the nerves, the thought of being caught by a random shell seemed always worse, more futile, than being slain in a storm shower of lead. Any cats that were around would have been scavenging strays, nervous and untrusting of the soldiers, dogs like Charlotte's small terrier would just as likely have been the prey of the hordes of rats as themselves being in hunting packs.

Above the fire a simple mantelpiece with yet more photographs. These clearly of more sentimental value as they were in tarnished silver frames and all held portraits of single people.

'My family,' Charlotte signalled her return, noticing where

Tommy's eyes had fallen. 'My mother, my father, my brother Dirk, my husband Peter and my children Clara and Dennis,' she pointed at the photographs in turn.

'Very lovely,' Tommy responded, not really sure how he should respond, and certainly not pleased with how he did. 'A lovely family,' he continued.

Charlotte placed a plate with a generous portion of pie onto the seat beside Tommy, ignoring his comments and offering him a fork.

'Enjoy, it is fresh, still warm,' she commented.

Tommy took the fork and picked up the plate. He cut a chunk of the pie with the side of the fork, skewered it and put it in his mouth. The taste of apples was subtly infused with cinnamon; he chewed, savoured and swallowed. It was the best food that he had eaten for longer than he could imagine. Warm, sweet and full of flavour, it melted in his mouth and slid down his throat. As he finished up the last morsel on his plate the generosity of the helping suddenly didn't seem so great.

'Thank you, that was…' he searched for the word. 'Wonderful,' he said offering the plate back to his hostess. It was a poor choice of word; it didn't encapsulate in any way how the food made him feel.

'I shall get you some more,' Charlotte declared.

'No, no, I am fine, thank you,' Tommy replied.

'Of course, you are hungry, there is plenty, I'll return.' Charlotte was clear and decisive in her words, and immediately strode out of the room, not giving Tommy any opportunity to reject her hospitality.

He relaxed into her sofa and watched the cat lick its paw and then brush it over its ear. It was a slow, methodical motion that it repeated over and over. Tommy's eyes began to grow heavier, hypnotized by the actions of the feline. When she returned with the cake Charlotte found him deeply asleep, his arms crossed in his lap and his chin lolled down onto his chest.

She smiled and tutted, mock chastisingly, then took a small blanket that lay on the headrest of the armchair, unfolded it and placed it over his body.

'Sleep well Tommy,' she whispered, and beckoning the dog out with her she left the Englishman to rest.

At six thirty the next morning Tommy was at Hell Fire Corner.

He had slept well, twice. The second time in his new room in a bed that was a great improvement to the one he had back home in England. Charlotte's apple pie was the best thing he had eaten in years until he had gone down the next morning and found a feast of cheeses, meats, porridge, breads and fruit laid out on the long dining table. She told him that there was plenty for all, though 'the others' wouldn't be down for a half hour or so, so he was to feel welcome to fill his belly and then grab whatever he wanted to take to consume whilst he was working. Charlotte even provided him with a brown paper bag to put it all in.

Tommy had known exactly how to find Hell Fire Corner, even with the whole landscape changed his sense of direction was keen. During the war it had been infamous for the danger that it presented just outside the confines of Ypres, a crossroads that the German guns kept fixed in their sites. Only the massive muslin cloths erected by the Allies gave any form of protection by shielding the numbers of troops passing through at any given time. In the last year of the war, when the Germans were pressing for victory in March, Hell Fire Corner was one of the rallying points in the Ypres Salient where the enemy were arrested in their advances, the point where the tide began to turn for a final time.

As Tommy approached the corner, he saw in front of him a small, rounded stone mound on his side of the road. The closer that he got, the more he was able to pick out finer details of the tiny obelisk. The top of the stone was sculpted in the form of a steel helmet, around the bottom, Mills bombs were on each corner and on the front was engraved "Ypres" and then "Here the invader was brought to a standstill, 1918, Hell Fire Corner".

Tommy set himself down on the verge beside the marker and prepared to wait for Alf. After just a few moments he noticed another figure ambling down towards him. As he neared, he looked at Tommy, deliberately caught his eye and nodded in welcome. Then, without saying a word he too sat down, a few feet from Tommy and began to eat an apple that he had taken out of his coat pocket. Then more men arrived, some singly, some in twos. Some were quiet and insular like the first, silently greeting with their eyes, a slight smile or a wave of the hand, others were more energised and gregarious, loudly proclaiming their arrival and warmly acknowledging others that they knew. By the time that Alf arrived there were perhaps fourteen or fifteen of them waiting. It was a mixed gathering with a multitude of accents. Most of them were British Tommy ascertained as he identified a thick Glasgow brogue, a gentle Black Country lilt, a Welsh valleys sing-song, the clearly identifiable but difficult to understand Tyneside, the loud and irresistibly friendly scouse and the harsh, angled voice from Belfast. There were those too who spoke English but with a more local Flemish tang and even perhaps he picked up two chatting quietly with each other in French, which could have made them either Ypres locals or from below the national border. Tommy had listened and observed keenly, trying to understand the picture that the men painted, to guess at their stories, to see how he fitted in with the collage.

Though their accents differed and clearly their personalities varied, they were still all of a type, a type that Tommy realised that he too was a part of. All these men had experienced life. Their quiet eyes or their laughing mouths, their heads angled down or their shoulders erect, they all bore their experiences differently, but the weight was shared by all. None, Tommy would say were over fifty, most were close to his age, none were boys. The only one that he struggled to place was the man that had been the first to arrive. He spoke to no-one, though he would occasionally acknowledge a wave or a nod, and his eyes barely raised themselves above his eyebrows. Tommy sensed a strength that was carrying a great burden, a pain suffered quietly, a loneliness. He was compelled to introduce himself, just to this quiet individual. He put out his hand.

'Tommy,' he said.

The man gripped it silently and said nothing. It was a solid handshake but nothing else. He didn't offer a name.

When Alf picked out Tommy, he headed straight for him and Tommy rose to take the man's hand.

'Good to see you Tommy,' he said smiling, looking straight into his eyes. Then, without introducing Tommy to the group, he turned and headed towards the rising sun along the Zonnebeke Road. As one, the contingent followed him.

They walked for a little over an hour until finally Alf raised his arm and stopped. Like a well-trained company the men pulled up behind him and awaited their orders. Alf took the rucksack that he was carrying from his back and placed it carefully on the ground, then resting down onto his haunches he opened it. He looked round at the men and made a point of counting them twice, then counted out from the sack a number of pencils and clipboards and a thick wad of paper. Having raised himself back to his feet, he wandered amongst the men handing them a pencil and board each and a ration of the paper. He chatted to each individually, sometimes asking a question, other times just making a simple greeting. He left Tommy until last, then before he handed over the last pencil, paper and board he announced loudly a list of numbers with the odd letter. It was a list that Tommy understood and identified instantly as co-ordinates, which he assumed represented where they stood. The men scribbled on the paper that they had attached to their boards and then quietly stepped a few paces forward into the field that lay before them. Without discussion they each found themselves a place in a line with just a few feet separating themselves from each other. Then they stood, invariably lit up a cigarette or pipe and waited for their orders.

Alf turned to Tommy and handed him his items, then looked him in the eyes, sincerity written over his countenance.

'We're here for the lads Tommy. To bring them home. We scour these fields looking for any sign that they're there. Sometimes it might be a hint of tunic fabric or the dull glint of a button or cap badge. Sometimes you'll just see the white of a bone. You'll find it difficult to begin with, but you'll get your eye in, then you'll be away. It's no race and there's no quota, just keep your eyes to the ground and do your bit for them. When you think you've found something stick your hand in the air to signal me, then see if you can brush the dirt away. If it's a lad, or part of a lad, I'll give you the exact co-ordinates of where you found him and you write it down on your paper. We'll mark the spot and we'll then see what we have got. Don't expect much, some days are more fruitful than others, but we're still bringing them in every day, even now. They're not often whole, but what there is we take care of. Does all of that make sense to you?'

Tommy nodded and wrote down the co-ordinates that Alf had called out that he had instinctively memorised.

'Good,' said Alf. 'Then join the line at the far end and try to fall in with the pace. We keep about two yards between us and when we reach the wood at the far end, we'll pivot round and come back. Ok?'

'Yes, I understand,' replied Tommy and he walked to the end of the line. Behind him Alf had put a whistle to his lips, then he blew. For a moment Tommy was back in the trenches and a sudden lurch hit his stomach, sweat instantly forming in the nape of his neck. But then he returned to the present and he set his eyes to the ground and became a searcher, a part of a rescue party, desperately looking for anyone that needed to find their way home.

He was aware that first morning that he was walking at a slower pace than the others, but it didn't trouble him, he was the new lad here and he needed to find his step. His inexperienced eyes sought harder and scrutinised more carefully the ground at his feet. Often, he would perceive a dew glistening stone to be the shine of a badge, or a clump of foliage the hint of material. Occasionally he would be aware of the hand of a colleague rising to the air and a corresponding flurry of activity, but his eyes picked out only masquerades. At the wood the line of men pivoted around Tommy so that he stepped just a few feet to his left and turned round, but the one who had been on his far right moved furthest and remained most distant from Tommy. The pace was slow and relentless, but Tommy found that he had settled into the monotony with ease. Apart from pausing every now and again to windmill his arms and loosen his neck, he found that he became lost in his occupation. He was aware of the birds, the occasional motor car and the men about him, but otherwise he was in his own peaceful sphere and his mind felt deeply at ease. That first morning he found no sign of one of the fallen, though he did find a whole feast of remnants of the days of conflict. A five nine shell cone was the first that he noticed and from curiosity and a natural boy's instinct he brushed it clean and popped it in his pocket, then he found strands of barbed wire, bullet shell casings both with and without their bullets, rifling bands, countless shrapnel balls and a Mills bomb. Despite the passage of time and evidence that it had been well farmed, the ground was still littered with the fallout of battle and it made him consider how much had been spent over those years, both financially and physically.

Just before midday they broke for a rest and gathered together at the road's verge.

'What do we do with these?' Tommy asked openly but towards Alf as he produced the Mills bomb that he had stuck in his jacket pocket. Most of the men looked to see what he was alluding to and in satisfying themselves merely resumed the consuming of their food and drink. Alf headed to him, talking as he did so.

'Anything like that just leave by the roadside, it gets collected. You'll see plenty of it I promise you. It's pretty harmless unless you hit it with a plough or strike it with a spade. There's always a few that get done by them each year, mostly farmers out with their horses in the spring, and there's plenty of stories of bombs being harvested as potatoes. Just be careful of the gas shells, they can be nasty, some of them have started to erode and leak. You don't want any of that stuff near you, as well you know.'

Tommy placed the bomb down by the base of a tree and sat down, stretching out his legs in front of him. He found himself once again next to his first colleague. He raised his eyebrows in acknowledgement, then taking two apples from his pack offered him one. The man's eyes looked deeply into Tommy's as if he was looking for an answer and then took the apple offered to him.

'Thank you,' he muttered quietly.

'I didn't catch your name,' Tommy said.

The man looked again at Tommy, stared into his eyes as if judging the situation but said nothing. His eyes dropped for a moment, almost in embarrassment, then rose again to meet Tommy's. There was a solidity about his stare, almost a defiance, then he opened his mouth and said one word. 'Hans.' He held Tommy's eyes judging the reaction.

'Good to meet you Hans, I'm Tommy as I said this morning.' Tommy wiped his hand on his trousers and offered it. Hans took it firmly and gave a brief nod, then turned back to his apple and bit deeply into it.

Tommy had sensed that there was something about Hans, though he couldn't quite put his finger on what it was. There was a weight being carried that seemed to surpass anyone else's there and he was conspicuously a loner. He hadn't guessed that he was German, but that abrupt syllable was unmistakeable in its delivery. Tommy had for a moment felt a shock of surprise, but then instantly felt that his questions had been answered. The wall around Hans was a defence against enquiries and prejudices which would surely be fired at him if his nationality was widely known. Acceptance wasn't something that Hans expected.

It would subsequently take Tommy months to learn Hans' motivations for putting himself in the most incongruous setting possible. The German's history would be divulged piecemeal as half sentences, fragmented memories and anecdotes during innumerable journeys to fields to be cleared, breaks in their workday and eventually late-night drinking sessions.

Hans Schmidtke had always dreamed of following in his father's footsteps and to serve his country. The stories that the older Schmidtke had regaled to his son were filled with acts of courage, men of honour and days filled with excitement from his experiences of the Franco-Prussian War. Enthusiastically he would tell how he would man his Krupp cannon, a finer gun than anything the French had to offer, and systematically aim and destroy the enemy. He had tales of Gravelotte and Metz where he escaped injury and death by the merest of whiskers, and then how he was struck by French artillery fire at the Siege of Paris. There at the French capital he had lost days of his life being knocked senseless from their enemy fire, when he eventually awoke in a poorly provisioned field hospital, he discovered with horror that an arm and a leg had been ripped from him.

To Hans, his father had been his hero from the very earliest days of his childhood. The wounds that he had sustained were badges of honour and Hans would go on to retell his father's stories, pride shining in his eyes with every word spoken, to his friends at school and church.

Hans studied hard throughout his young life, never being diverted, like so many of his peers, by sports or girls, always clearly focussed on his ambitions. He simply wanted to follow in his father's footsteps and be the son that all in his family would be proud of. By the time war clouds were forming in Western Europe and the Schlieffen Plan was finally about to be thrust against the Low Countries, Hans had created something of a name for himself in military circles. He had mercilessly and speedily forced his way through the lower ranks to become one of the youngest Oberleutnants of the Empire, excelling in every discipline that he was introduced to. He was uniformly admired by his superior officers and loved by the men that served him. He was naturally a modest man, a strict but fair commander and a hardworking soldier that would never ask another to do a job that he wouldn't do.

Hans loved his men as every truly great leader does, treating and thinking of them as family, but he loved the guns that they operated more, the guns were his babies, and he took pride and responsibility in each and every one of them.

When Hans lost a man to enemy fire, or as was often the case, to an accident, he would mourn him and ensured that all in his company paid the respects to him that he was due. When he saw any of his guns destroyed, he would take it as a personal affront and was often inconsolable in his self-chastisement. He was proud of his armaments in the same way that his father had been of his, in Hans' mind they were both blessed with having been guardians of the finest pieces of artillery of their respective generations. Always, the letters that he wrote back to his family extolled the virtues of his charges and subsequently the greatness of the German cause and the honour he personally felt in following a family tradition.

The war to Hans was a beautiful embodiment of his life's dreams. Day in, day out he felt that he was doing exactly what he had been born to do. His guns were always the best maintained in the entire army and were often hailed as examples to other companies and regiments. The men under Hans' command were the most disciplined and the hardest working. The deadly accuracy that they produced together manning their guns was remarked upon at High Command, questioned how it was possible, and extolled as achievements that all artillery sections should be able to attain.

Throughout the long campaign of the war Hans was offered

promotions that would take him out of the lines, often to a safer life. He was so admired that his superiors felt that his talents would be used to greater effect instructing others in his skills back behind the lines. To all these great compliments, Hans politely declined. His place, he felt, would always be with his men and his guns.

Hans led a blessed existence throughout the conflict, even though the Allies sought to annihilate the artillery of their enemy and the men that worked it, time and time again he escaped meaningful injury. There would be few who would be able to boast as many days in the lines as Hans, fewer still who would come away unscathed as he did. He became a legendary figure to those that knew him and served with him, many seeing him as a good luck charm, others referring to him as an almost inhuman machine that was just like the guns that he adored so much.

Hans was a meticulous officer who knew exactly how many shells his unit had fired in each hour of each day. He would always seek out confirmation of the success or failure of their efforts from whatever observers were available, whether they were in balloons, aeroplanes or church towers. When he, his men and his guns dropped below the great standards that he set for them all, he would trawl through all the facts at his disposal to understand the reasons why, then regardless of the effort or time that it would take him, he would correct the situation so that they did not fail on the next occasion.

When Hans' guns bore great success, he praised his men heartily, but in such a manner that they understood that they should feel momentary pride, but conceit would never be condoned, and failure was just one poor aim ahead of them. Success had to be consistent, not occasional and any soldier that did not appreciate the seriousness of his intention was soon dispelled and sent to another, less concerned unit.

Whilst those fighting in the front trenches saw death in graphic, daily detail, Hans saw comparatively little of it. He saw those around him destroyed when the British guns occasionally got lucky or the French had had a rare, good day, and sometimes witnessed the corpses of both sides as the guns pushed forwards to the coast, or retreated back to the east. Rarely did he see the death of his enemy from his own actions. Never did he see his enemy as men like himself with families and dreams, that laughed and sang and farted. The enemy was faceless. An objective. Inhuman. Less than machine.

The day that his perceptions were changed about his enemy was the day that his war was effectively finished.

The whole German army knew that it was the last throw of the dice. A do or die situation to finish the Allies off now or face the inevitable defeat. 1917 had given them a welcome and morale raising boost when the Revolution in Russia had brought peace on the Eastern Front and thus the opportunity for the great German war machine to muster along one front, in the West against the Allies. Spring 1918 was the opportunity, the last one left to them to throw everything possible at a final victory.

It wasn't just the impending arrival of the Americans that made it clear to soldiers at every level that the war was being lost, it was also the news of those starving back home in Germany, the depletions of their own food rations and the gradual denudation of quality of their resources and armaments. Hans had noticed the first time that shells arrived that were not up to grade, certainly not up to his grade. He could see the signs and understood what they meant, that the war would be lost sooner rather than later if tactics weren't changed. For too long the Germans had been embedded into their thickly constructed concrete fortifications, soaking up the rain of fire that was sent to them. In the summer of 1914, they had shown what German aggression could achieve; now in the minds of all those like Hans, it was their time and their duty to seize the initiative again, to force the British into the sea and emasculate the Belgians and French forever. The German Empire had one more chance and it was imperative that it took it.

It would become known as the Spring Offensive. The Kaiserschlacht. But before it was noted in history books, when it was just a set of orders and commands coming down the lines, the operation excited Hans with its clear ambition and energy. This was the great thrust that he had believed was the only course of action and it was going to be realised, he would throw every sinew of his body to achieve his part in the success.

When it came, when that massive push was put into action and the Allies instantly began to buckle at the intensity of the attacks, the command that Hans gave was relentless and remorseless. His company without exception was the most forcibly energetic. With each explosive retort from his guns Hans could taste success in his mouth, as his guns pounded the enemy lines, the infantry pushed on, grabbing great swathes of new territory. Then with each storming success his guns would be partially dismantled and pushed forward to new standings closer to Ypres, to the coast, to victory. The news from in front of them was of constant advance, the enemy lines were being expunged, they were punching through, annihilating all in their path. It was clearly only a matter of time and the mood amongst the artillery was one of celebration.

Then gradually the mood began to change. As the rapid advances slowed and the expected victory didn't materialise, stories began to filter down the lines, back to the gunners at the rear, back to the ears of Hans. At first, he ignored what he heard, he could see that the progresses that they had made which were at first so rapid, were bound to be stalled quite naturally. The pace that the infantry had set could simply not be kept up with by the massive guns that he commanded. His guns were moved at a painful pace, constantly held back by the thick mud that they sunk into. To remain a supportive force for the army the guns had to keep up, but it was a simple fact that they struggled to do so.

The stories however wouldn't go away, they spread like tentacles backwards from the front, and like all rumours they became the truth in the minds of the men that heard them repeatedly. They were a constant whisper that gnawed away at the morale causing anger and dissatisfaction.

Hans wouldn't allow himself to believe the mutterings, they were a nonsense that he wouldn't acknowledge.

He was prepared to believe that the enemy trenches that were being overrun were indeed filled with the kinds of treasures that the German forces had for months only been able to dream about. It was perfectly feasible with the access to the ports, the control the Allies held over the seas and with the support in particular of the Americans that their trenches could indeed contain great quantities of provisions like the wine, chocolate, sugar and meat that was being spoken of. What Hans wouldn't accept was the unpatriotic suggestions that the great advance was being held up, not only because of the immobility of the guns, but also, and more importantly, because of the gluttony and weakness of the advance soldiers who had been suddenly confronted with these stores of delight. It was being said that these soldiers were attacking the stores with even greater aggression than they had been attacking the enemy. That they had thrown themselves with greed at the bounty, devouring and imbibing with scant regard to the military orders to advance, advance, advance. These men, it was being suggested, were creating drunken and slovenly companies that were unfit for battle and were even refusing to push on being seduced so much by the spoils that they had uncovered.

Hans refused to believe the murmurs, but just the fact that they were being repeated angered and appalled him, the very suggestion that any German soldier could behave in such a disgraceful manner ripped into his sensibilities. As he found his great cannons emasculated by the mud, stuck too far from the front lines to be of any practical use, Hans became determined to throw himself into the melee, as a warrior. He gave no orders for his men to join him, but instructed them of his decision, he was going to enter the epicentre of the war and engage the enemy man to man.

All of those under his command listened to and comprehended his decision, then as he saluted, turned and marched from them, they stood and followed him wordlessly to venture into the trenches and to the fury.

The first trenches that they came upon were in good shape. They were their own trenches and appeared hardly damaged, the diligence of the German construction evident. Then they emerged from what had previously been the Front Line to cross over the space that had for so long been the No Man's Land between the armies. This was a chaotic, crater filled expanse of churned up mud, wire and death. The Germans had advanced so quickly over this terrain that they hadn't had the time to collect their own dead or dignify them with any form of internment. Ubiquitously the corpses of Hans' own army lay strewn, misshapen and disarrayed by the bullets from the trenches that they sought. Some were fractured beyond recognition, others draped over the barbed wire like rugs on a washing line, most were bloated, putrefying freely in the open air. These proud Prussians, some of the greatest to have served the Kaiser, had been annihilated by the panicked guns of the British in the trenches that faced them. Their forms had seemed huge and monstrous, to those men stood on the firesteps with fear gripping their stomachs and sweat pouring over their palms. The ones that had reached the parapets had jumped down with banshee wails, shooting and bayoneting any that they discovered there. The British had faced them, fought them and been destroyed by them and the advance had commenced. But the bodies that Hans and his men were picking through had seen none of that glory, their time had come too soon and now their silent screams and harried bodies filled him with a greater anger and firmer determination. His strides lengthened, his jaw was set, his hands gripped his rifle with a greater purpose and belief. Hans was now in pursuit of the enemy.

They too got to the parapets of the British trenches just as their comrades had done but they were barely recognisable as a forward defence. The little that had survived the destruction made by the Prussians and the shells of his own guns had been modified and turned by the advancing Germans so that what had once been a parapet against them was now a parados, and the parados now their own parapet. They climbed and slid down to the trench floor. It was a dishevelled and chaotic mess that met them. Splintered wooden frames sprawled haphazardly amongst the sandbags that had been pushed and blown from their perches. It was an angry scene filled with the stench of rotting flesh. Caught below the surface the stink of death struck Hans and his men like a body blow and momentarily they all reeled from the shock of it. Instinctively they covered their mouths and noses with their hands then began to pick their way through the destruction that had awaited them. The dead here were predominantly their enemy, dressed in khaki, smaller and less impressive than their own countrymen. They pushed through, seeking the route to the battle.

The trenches were a maze, sodden with rain, blood and the dead. The further in that they delved, the newer the dead became, the more lifelike, the less grotesque in their decay. Some could have been wax effigies; others could have been sleeping. These dead were increasingly the enemy. Those killed in their attempts to defend until they could retreat and escape.

As he passed the decaying humanity, Hans couldn't fail to feel his heart soften. The faces that looked back at him began to bear souls, histories, characters. He began to notice their youth and the lives that they should have led.

But still he took his men forward, still he had belief in his purpose. The trenches that had once been the front line dissolved into communication trenches leading to the second and third lines. At times the dead had become mounds that in order to advance they had to climb and crawl over. Other times the trenches were clear as if some great machine had been through, clearing a path. Then finally they emerged from the gutters back onto the surface.

They were now at the back of the old British front lines, Ypres lay in front of them albeit at a distance. The sounds of combat were clear, no longer a muddy, indiscernible collage of noise, now they could hear the individual reports of rifles and spatterings of machine guns in front of them. The moans and screams of the afflicted were tangible amongst shouts of command and support. Hans and his men were close to the battle line and it didn't sound to him that the Germans were fighting with anything less than pride and fervour.

Their boots trod into the mud and Hans realised that this was the sector that he had been fixated on so diligently for so long. It had been his suggestion and it had been approved by those far above him, that if they could destroy their enemy when most vulnerable in retreat, then they would surely win the war. Co-ordinates were assessed and given out. Gun projections were calculated, recalculated and then agreed upon. The guns would almost be firing at their limit, so accuracy was of utmost importance. Hans had slaved over his figures; he had taken everything into account, and he had come up with degrees and angles that he felt were unquestionable. Everything had been geared for full destruction of the enemy in an exact area of co-ordinates. It had all been scientific and mathematical, at no point had faces or personalities been put onto the enemy; that was the intent of the destruction.

The co-ordinates that had become so much a part of his life for such a short time now projected into the mind of Hans. They were clear and definable, white markings on a blackboard that stood behind his eyes. The numbers became a grid on a map, the map became the land, and that land became the reality that held them in that moment.

It was a field of unqualified success. The degree of mastery, the perfection of aim was unquestionable, the achievement undeniable. These were meadows that evoked supreme soldiering. Trophies were given for creating scenes such as what lay before them. It was scholarly in its exactitude, professorial. Evidence of Hans' genius. It was his finest hour, his finest epitaph.

Before them natural ground cover no longer existed. Grass, bushes, trees, mud, even stone and rock were all devoid. The pasture was simply of tunic, steel, bone and flesh. It was a perfect landscaped acreage of war.

Hans stopped and surveyed his masterpiece. Completely aware that this was his doing, the fruit of his skill. In that moment, that one single breath, the war of Hans Schmidtke ended. Like an electrically charged shock to his brain he convulsed, then vomited and collapsed down to his knees sobbing.

'Wer bin ich? Was habe ich gemacht?' he uttered.

His men surrounded him, shocked by this unfamiliar show of emotion and humanity. They tried to console him, to bring him to his feet and cajole him back onto their path, but he turned to them with fury, a cat trapped in a corner. He whipped out his Mauser pistol and threatened them all with it, screaming incoherently. As one they backed away, their hands raised not in surrender but acceptance. Then Hans placed the gun to his head and pulled the trigger.

He was back behind the German lines when his eyes reopened. Ironic that the exactitude of his preparations to kill others was not mirrored in his ability to destroy himself. It was the pain in his head that had brought him back to consciousness, a tapping of hundreds of toffee hammers on his temple. The pain made him retch, bringing him to the attention of the nurse. Her face was professionally impassive. She jostled him back onto his back and administered something to him without uttering a word. He felt a fog and morphia again consumed him.

As he slept, he dreamt of marshes and swamps of dismembered limbs and torsos, faces without eyes, eyes without faces, mouths wide open in silent screams, hands crawling and grasping at him as he tried to navigate through. Each time that he awoke, escaping back into the world away from his dreams, he felt the pounding of the guns in his head and the visions stayed with him.

Hans never escaped his nightmares. They remained with him when he returned to his home and family, and when he tried to study as an engineer. They were there when he lay with his new bride and later when she was heavy with their child. Eventually he succumbed to them and took his penance. He walked from his marital home and his eighteen-month-old daughter without explanation, just kissing both the ladies in his life one last time, leaving an apology in the air that he knew would never be enough for the wrongs that he was doing to them. It was, however, the only course of action that he could envision that would ever give him peace. He returned to Belgium and to the area that had once been the Ypres Salient, there he headed for the German Cemetery at Langemark. His energies and strength were welcomed in that desolate graveyard that held the bodies of thousands from his country who had not survived. But it wasn't amongst his own that he saw his place. He remained there only until he learnt the name of Alf Barnes, the Englishman who daily toiled in the sector searching for the lost souls. Hans sought him out and approached him one night in a bar in Poelkapelle. Alf hadn't needed any explanation; he saw in the man's eyes the pain that needed healing and simply told him to be at Hell Fire Corner the next morning.

In helping to seek out those who remained strewn across the fields of Flanders, Hans had given himself a purgatorial sentence, but it also gave him a release from his visions and a hope of reconciliation.

For Tommy, the rest of that first day alongside Hans, Alf and the other stalwarts was fruitless, nevertheless without question he re-joined them the next day and the next, and many successive days after. At the end of each day's work Alf would tell them where they would meet the following morning. Often it would be at Hell Fire Corner, sometimes it was nearer Hooge, or occasionally further north at Poelcapelle, or down towards Essex Farm. Those that joined the ranks would periodically change, new faces would take over from those that had moved on, but the task always remained the same. A methodical seeking of the lost.

And the lost would be found.

Tommy found his first soul on his second day, the clue in the dirt had been part of the lad's tunic. It was hardly more than a fragment, but it caught Tommy's eye and caused him to bend down and investigate. He brushed the mud away and delved into the soil, not really expecting to discover anything of importance. There was a humerus beneath the cloth which then led to a clavicle bone. His discovery shocked him, and he fell backwards off his haunches and in doing so raised and waved his hand more frantically than he would have wanted.

With Alf at his side, they gently unearthed remains that were almost complete and even a novice like Tommy could ascertain that the hole in the skull would most likely have been the cause of death. His identity would never be discovered, but to Tommy that didn't matter, he had brought some lad back to the world, whoever he was, he was no longer lost.

After his first, Tommy's second, third and fourth came in quick succession, then it was almost a conveyor belt of success.

He would sometimes say that he could hear them calling to him from just below the surface, then his eyes would catch a flash of brass or a hint of bone. Sometimes what he would unearth would be the bones of a lad that appeared as if he had just laid down peacefully, in sleepful repose without a mark on him to imply a violent end. Other times it would be an angry mash of bones thrown chaotically together, two, three or four bodies intertwined in their moment of death. On one occasion Tommy merely uncovered a boot, that still held its wearer's foot within it. Whatever he found, whatever was unearthed, it was always treated in exactly the same manner. With dignity and respect.

Once that first indication was confirmed, whatever remains lay beneath the ground would be gently revealed with the mud and dust being carefully brushed away. Hessian sacks would be placed on the ground by the side of the small trench that they had created and then, with infinite care, all that was found would be taken out of their lost space and placed within.

Regardless of how many days later it would be, Tommy was always there at the simple ceremony that honoured those bones. Now resting in a plain box coffin, they were brought to the chosen cemetery and with little fuss, no pomp, but much dignity, they were interred with a few words spoken, to rest along with their brothers in arms.

Tommy never failed to pay his respects and always left with a sense of pride in what had been achieved for all the boys. It was gardens, not cemeteries, that they were being laid to rest in. With flowers, bushes, trees and birds singing in the skies. Places that could be openly visited and where visitors would be welcomed. It was Fabian Ware's great vision and Tommy embraced the whole enterprise and his tiny part within it. Tommy knew that Fabian Ware had foreseen the importance of creating suitable resting places for the boys, gardens that would pay tribute to them, but also pay tribute to all that had been over there. Gardens that families could feel at peace in. It was a mission that had to be correct in every detail and Tommy knew, with each additional garden that he witnessed, that it was a project that had been done right and one in which he felt an innate pride.

Tommy worked in the fields around Ypres for almost three years, but then he had sought and been given a position tending one of the gardens, to look after the carpets and furnishings of these tiny corners of foreign fields that would always be, to him at least, a little bit of Britain. The garden that he had been given was the largest, he had heard, of all the British gardens. It had been named Tyne Cot after the nickname of the machine gun posts that were situated within it. Machine gun posts that had caused such destruction to the Imperial Forces in the autumn of 1917 as they had tried to push outwards from Ypres to liberate the tiny village of Passchendaele. It was a beautiful garden and Tommy was proud to work there. It had quickly become his life, he felt that it was his calling to be there.

Tommy had a wonderful sense of peace working amongst the headstones. There were almost 12,000 of them, a division, with the majority facing up the incline to the Sword of Sacrifice as if in attention to their commanding officer. In that great division of headstones most had their identities lost to the world, they were now only known unto God.

And now, Tommy had started a new daily habit, each day he would proudly pass from one end to the other of the huge back wall that had recently been built and unveiled. A great wall that hosted the names of 35,000 of those that hadn't been found, or at least not been identified. Some of those lying unknown in the confines of Tyne Cot, would surely have their names on that wall, Tommy would think to himself as he walked along it each day, actively reading out a name at intervals. Whether their bodies had been found or not, these lads, lost in the Ypres Salient in the latter months of the war were not forgotten. They were here, imprinted in the masonry to be remembered in perpetuity.

Tommy read different names each day, choosing different panels to focus on, but then he would always finish with the panel that held the one name that meant so much to him. The name to which he could put a face and a voice and a history.

Tommy felt deep within him that his son was not just present on the wall, but that he was there, within the garden, amongst the division. He was sure of it. Sometimes, Tommy felt that he rested near the side wall, under the tree by the old bunker. Other times he would be close to the front gate. And other times he would be back behind the sword, by the Germans that were incongruous in their presence.

He had been lost at the beginning of November 1917 somewhere on the slope that led to Passchendaele. They never knew exactly when, the 2nd perhaps or maybe the 3rd, it was not long before that great action was finally halted.

Tommy had been there at the same time, but he had had no idea that his son was even across the Channel, let alone so close to him. Had he known, then maybe he could have saved him, maybe he could have shielded him from the shell, taken the bullet for him, or dragged him from the mud. If only he had known. It was of course a ridiculous notion, but it was the thought that had plagued Tommy every single day since the moment he had discovered that he could have been within feet or yards of his dying son. And of all places to be lost, of all times, Third Ypres.

It had all started so well, or so it seemed. The beginning of summer in 1917, Tommy had witnessed along with the rest of his company, the sequence of massive explosions that had literally blown the Germans off the Messines Ridge. Explosions from the ammonal that had been so carefully placed in deep cavities beneath the Germans, cavities created from the painstaking work of months and months of miners and engineers gouging out tunnels beneath No Man's Land, worming into enemy territory.

Tommy was in Poperinge, out of the lines, about ten miles west of Ypres, but still very much in the sector, when the mines were blown. It was an early June morning, the previous night he had enjoyed a bath, and freshly laundered clothes, then had first called in to TocH and afterwards watched an old Charlie Chaplin film shown at the cinema. It was a good break out of the lines, and he was enjoying it immensely, the blowing of the mines rounded it off perfectly.

It was a thunderous and gargantuan effect that shook the ground, even in Poperinge. For those like Tommy that were prepared for the explosions it was a shock and a surprise, frightening beyond belief to begin with, but then as news filtered slowly around and the cloud in the distance pointed out, fears reduced, and hopes were raised. The cloud that seemed to hang all over the German lines to Tommy's eyes was a dirty fog, not even tangible of any particular colour, but a fog that hung and then fell. Barely perceptible at such a distance, but those closer would claim they could see the limbs and heads, helmets, rocks, mud, guns and everything else raining back down on the enemy. Word spread like wildfire that this was the big one. This was the winning of the war. The Germans could not come back from this one. They would all be in Berlin by tea-time!

In the Front Lines the men followed up on the explosions, knowing that the great advance would soon happen. Out of the lines, in Poperinge where Tommy stood, the excited air was inhaled by them all. They all concluded that this would be the moment when they would be rushed to the Front to strike the winning blows. Tommy readied himself for the inevitable call.

But it never came.

Despite his own preparedness and that of all the men around him, despite the follow up by those already in the lines, the orders never came to make the great advance, the advance that they felt would smash the enemy to pieces. The orders instead were to hold tight, stay prepared but wait for reinforcements.

Tommy wasn't alone in feeling the frustration. He could see, as they all could see that this was the great opportunity and if they didn't make use of it then it would be lost, possibly forever. What reinforcements did they need? None, Tommy had felt. Screw them, just blow the whistles and let them finish the job while they could.

But they refused to blow the whistles, and the command was reiterated that they were to wait, the Generals knew what they were doing, the reinforcements were on the way.

So, they waited.

Throughout the rest of June, they waited. Through most of July.

And while they waited it rained. It rained and it rained and it rained. Like nothing they could imagine in the height of summer. Tommy considered these weeks the worst imaginable. In due course he would reconsider that thought.

When finally, they were all told that the advance was imminent, it wasn't the thought of machine gun bullets ripping into his body that terrified Tommy. It was the mud. The thick, cloying, sodden mud that they would be asked to climb out of the trenches into.

The shrill whistles blew all down the line, and locked in his own personal bubble, Tommy climbed up the trench ladder and onto the parapet. Immediately the rattle of the German guns was all around them, and they stepped purposefully forward with jelly filled legs. A scream to his right broke into Tommy's consciousness and he glanced across. Six feet, maybe seven feet from him Dick Evans, a thick set man with hands like dinner plates and eyebrows that joined in the middle, had been struck by burning metal. It was clearly only a nick though, somewhere just above his knee. Tommy saw it all, time slowing for the performance. Dick's knee buckled with the strike and sent him to his knees, surprise in his eyes but not panic. He glanced at Tommy and their eyes met, they both knew that it was nothing serious, that chances were Dick had a blighty one and would be safe home for a while. Tommy even believed that he saw Dick wink at him, though it could have just been dirt thrown into his eye. Then the big man was being pushed down horizontally into the mud. The weight of the pack on his back forcing his torso down, his knee unable to offer support with the severed tendons above it. Into the mud he was thrust, his face, his head, his chest. The pack looking like a tombstone above him. Dick's arms flailed in an attempt to find a purchase to push himself back out, to right himself, to pull his way back to the sanctuary of the trenches. The flailing gathered pace; momentum fuelled by panic.

Tommy watched in horror and despair. He hadn't known Dick long, just a passing acquaintance really. A familiar face, nothing more. Tommy shared his torment but was a hopeless observer with no chance of saving the situation. So close, but in that thick slurry of mud, too far. He watched the man slowly drown, incapable of repositioning his mouth to safety or shifting the weight of his pack.

Tommy survived that day and every day following as they fought out of the lines and slowly, so slowly up the gradual incline which seemed like the sheerest face of an alpine mountain, towards that tiny village of Passchendaele. They fought for each inch through mud, each foot, each yard. On one occasion Tommy passed a lad caught in a shell hole, water up to the bottom of his tunic. His face was full of panic, terror glazed his eyes. At the rim of the hole, on their bellies, two or maybe three of his friends reached out to him with their hands or rifles, trying to pull him out to safety. Tommy passed on, hunched to the ground, seeking his own shell hole for safety.

A couple of days later Tommy passed that shell hole again, this time he was going the other way. The lad was still there. Now the water above his eye line.

Tommy never forgot that mud. He would always remember that for an eternity there was no escape from it. There were thousands of them trying to claw their own individual paths towards the German guns. They were commanded as units, they followed orders as units, but in reality, each minute of every day they were fighting their own very personal wars that had one unifying objective, to survive one more day.

They were obliterated all around him that autumn, some smashed by the shells, some by the maxims, all of them raped by the mud through which they attempted to traverse.

Tommy prevailed through nothing more than luck. He was no braver or more able than most of those that failed to survive. He was quite simply more fortunate.

The days were remorseless, the agony unremitting.

Thousands and thousands of them would succumb that autumn, and one of them was Tommy's son. Just another number, another statistic, another name to be mourned.

Tommy had begged his son not to join up. Letter after letter home he had repeated the words: "Son, when your time comes, when you are called up, then you must do your duty to your country, to your king, to yourself, and sign up. But DO NOT give your life away before time. Do not be in a rush to be over here." For a while Tommy's words had been heeded by his son and he had remained with his mother, living the sort of life a young man should be able to enjoy, but then one night he couldn't follow his father's commands any longer.

Alice would later write to Tommy telling him that their boy had been at a dance one night with a couple of his friends. They were all nice lads, brimming with youthful enthusiasm but not a bad bone amongst them. The dance had been at the Worker's Hall where there was a sprung floor. He had looked forward to going, it had become a highlight of his week, an escape from the mundanity of working in the shop. The boys had been minding their own business sat at the side of the hall, they had all been just enjoying the band, most likely enjoying the girls drifting by, possibly a little energised, but dangers to no one. Three young boys, enjoying life.

One of them noticed the girl stand up and nudged the others. She was a pretty thing who had been sitting at the far end of the hall almost exactly opposite them. They had all noticed her before and in their immaturity had joked about her long legs, pretty face and small, pert tits. No doubt she had calculated what they were laughing about because before she chose to stand, she glowered at them with unconfined menace. She strode to them with an intentional stride, keeping her eyes fixed solely on the three of them, then as she neared the group she focussed on Tommy's boy. He had shifted uneasily, one of his friends would later recount, and was unable to meet her stare until she was stood directly in front of him. He looked up into her narrowed eyes as she held herself there, statuesque in her poise. He coughed and mumbled something that no one either heard or remembered, then silently the girl unfurled her left fist revealing a white feather and handed it directly to the boy. Then she turned on the spot and paced back to her seat.

The very next day Tommy's son attested. A few short months after that he was sent over the Channel, then soon enough he had made the acquaintance of the Ypres Salient. He never got to experience much of the war, he was quickly thrown into the lines and sent into the mud beneath Passchendaele. He was still in the mud. The same mud that lay beneath Tommy's feet.

He was never found, or at least never identified. At seventeen years of age, he was just another victim of the politicians' war.

Seventeen. It would play on Tommy's mind over and over again. Just seventeen, it was no age. He knew his son wasn't unique in being one of the youthful dead, he was keenly aware that his boy wasn't the youngest. Valentine Strudwick who Tommy often went to visit down at Essex Farm Cemetery was just fifteen when he got it. Then there was of course John Condon at Poelcappelle, he was said to be only fourteen. But really did it make any difference? Fourteen, fifteen or seventeen, they were all too young. Hell, Tommy would think, twenty-seven was too young or thirty-seven or even sixty-seven like Henry Webber on the Somme, he was too young too.

Tommy knew full well that the tears that Henry Webber's missus and kids shed when they heard of his loss were the self-same tears that Tommy and Alice shed when their son was lost. They were all too young. All of them.

Tommy raked the leaves into a small pile and picked them up with two short planks of wood. When he was here his thoughts would often spiral out of control. Some days he was perfectly at peace, content to be a small part in the care of the gardens and the lads. Other days his mind was more agitated. The grief of losing his boy would still consume him and he would career down into the depths of his mind thinking about his war. He would torpedo from one recollection to another, all the time trying to find some reasoning behind it all. Some sanity. Some all-encompassing purpose that made their lives relevant.

He began to think of Henry Webber. Tommy hadn't known Henry, but he had known, at sixty-seven, that he was the oldest that had been lost. These things got known to the lads in the trenches. It was information that just filtered through, like whispered gossip, to them all. If he remembered right, if the gossip was accurate, Henry was lost at Mametz Wood on the Somme.

Tommy was there too, on the Somme. Of course he was, he had been everywhere, in one form or another tasting every delicacy that the Western Front had to offer. The Somme of 1916 he remembered with the clarity as if it had been only the previous week.

The guns had been incessantly pounding the Germans for days, weeks even. Hour after hour, day in, day out, a constant barrage of destruction. To Tommy, as with them all, the abuse of their own shells on their ears was unbearable, he couldn't imagine how it felt to be a German actually on the receiving end of the barrage. He knew it would have driven him absolutely mad.

The officers told them that the shells were winning the war, that not even a rat could survive what was being rained down on the German lines. NOT A RAT! And the barbed wire that separated the lines? It had all been destroyed they promised, completely flattened by the shrapnel shells. So, the officers went round proudly pronouncing to them all, when they were eventually sent over the top, when those whistles blew, they would have absolutely nothing to worry about. All they would need to do would be to climb up the ladders, step over the parapets and then walk steadily, resolutely and dignified like true English gentlemen, to the German lines and then quite simply and easily climb down into them and take possession. It would be as easy as that. Nothing to worry about. The war would be over, and they'd all be in Berlin by teatime.

Nobody wanted to question what the officers said. They were all so desperate to believe, that they did believe, Tommy certainly did.

He could recall the general mood as the day and the moment of the Great Offensive neared, it was almost euphoric, mixed with intense nervousness. Most of those who were going to be involved, so many of whom were Kitchener's, were energised to the point of irritation. Tommy remembered that there was a tendency to laugh longer and louder at inane jokes, for lads to beat each other on the back in joviality, and each and every one of them were totally restless, incapable of sitting still for even a moment.

Tommy had actually been disappointed when he was told that he wouldn't be amongst the first great wave out of their lines, he would have to wait a whole day before he could share in the glory. Even an old, experienced sweat like him, had been caught up in the buoyancy of the occasion. He, who knew what lies and deceptions were told to the ranks, still craved to believe.

Were they lies and deceptions then, as so many other times? He would often wonder in the years afterwards. Had the officers who spread the falsehoods believed in them, or was it endemic dishonesty? Maybe it was only the High Command who revelled in the great deceit? Or maybe it was none of them. Perhaps it was just poor intelligence that told of destroyed trench systems and obliterated wire.

Regardless of the truth it certainly didn't matter now, but how utterly stupid, naive and ignorant to allow themselves to believe that the enemy would, during a storm of shells, simply hang around and wait to be individually obliterated. The Germans had proven from the very beginning that they were a mighty army that was well commanded, disciplined and so often in greater control than their enemy were. Hadn't they, the Germans, when the trenches first began to be constructed, been the ones to grab the high ground at every opportunity, even if it had been at the expense of losing some ground? That elevation, that even when so moderate, would give them such a terrible advantage. They had rarely shown a weakness but had often displayed their mastery.

Those Germans knew from the outset what that great barrage had meant, they had probably been expecting it before the boys facing them had. They had been prepared. With the very first shells they had dived down into their dugouts, great concrete strongholds in which they knew they were as safe as could be expected. They locked themselves down there and simply waited for it to stop.

Had the British command not known that that was what they would do, Tommy often angrily thought, then they bloody well should have done.

Tommy would never forget the heat of that day when the first boys went over, it was clear that it was going to be a scorcher even before the sun was fully above the horizon. There was a shimmer of heat emanating above the morning dew making the land between the two armies appear like a gentle sea. The guns continued their cacophonous sound into the early morning, a fanfare to the coming action. Then there followed a definite sforzando as a string of mines were detonated beneath the Germans. Then silence. A complete vacuum of noise.

Tommy would say that that silence was as loud in his head as the gun reports had been, an out of place explosion of quiet.

And in the merest of moments, he swore that he did hear, high up in the French skies the joyful singing of a lark or possibly a meadow pipit.

Then the whistles blew, loud and long, and the lads jostled up the ladders to the top of the trenches.

That silence had been as deafening to the German ears, as it had been to Tommy's. They knew as one the danger that it signified. From their dugouts they stormed out to take to their firesteps and man their machine gun posts.

Then they waited for the inevitable.

They didn't wait for long.

Soon along the enemy lines in front of them they saw the emerging army. Heads, then shoulders, then bodies and legs rose as if from the bowels of the earth, and slowly, began to walk assuredly towards them. It was a long, snaking line of men being spewed out and sent towards them like a dreadful ooze intent on their destruction.

The Germans brought their rifles to their shoulders, manned their machine guns and took aim.

For a while, all that Tommy remembered hearing after the blowing of the whistles, was a jagged wall of sound. A murderous slicing of the air as countless rifles spat out their charges and burning machine gun lead rattled from one set of lines venomously to the other. It was a deluge of noise more urgent and furious than the constant baying of the artillery guns had been for so long.

Then gradually, sporadically, in amongst that wall of sound Tommy could pick out a scream, a human utterance of torment and hurt. Then it was less sporadic and more constant, until that was the only sound. To Tommy, the guns had fallen silent, all that he could hear was the agony of the lads. Some were short, staccato, reactive cries; the result of sudden pain, others were long drawn-out anguished moans. He could hear insistent, desperate calls for help over a tremolo of sobs and the pleading for water, for God, for mothers. Beneath it all there was one ensemble scream, continuous and breathless.

Throughout the day that symphony of misery continued as the sun beat down on them all. Long into the night the dreadful orchestra played. Even now, so many years later, Tommy would still wake up, sometimes suddenly, in the middle of the night, sweating profusely, with those cries and sobs filling his head. The agonies that had long been dispensed still echoed within him.

Then a little before dawn, it stopped. The music score ended. Or perhaps it was merely a tacet as the instruments prepared for the second movement. Regardless, the voices ceased even if the pain did not.

Tommy knew, that without fail, the next of kin of all those that fell for King and Country received simple letters usually from a commanding officer telling them that their son, or their husband or father had died courageously facing the German enemy. That their death had been quick and painless. That their actions were something to be proud of and to be taken heart from. None of those letters would ever say that their men had died slowly, drowned in the mud of Flanders or baked under the French sun. It was just as well, Tommy would always think, how could anyone possibly cope with knowing that that was how their lad had seen out their last moments?

So, Tommy was proud. He was proud to be where he was and doing what he was doing for the lads. His lads. He didn't have to be at Tyne Cot, he could be at any of the gardens, Thiepval Wood perhaps or Ploegsteert, Redan Ridge or Serre, or even at the hospital cemetery at Boulogne. It wouldn't matter, they were all the same to him, they were all his lads, and he was happy to do what was right by them. He knew that as a whole they weren't special; they were just ordinary blokes that happened to be caught up in extraordinary times. Some of them were indeed heroes who thought nothing about their own safe being, only the welfare of their friends and comrades, but others were far from heroic, cowards even, or men who would look the other way rather than stand up and be counted. They were the wonderful mix that is found in every generation, in every country, in every epoch. Some were the life and soul of every party, some were morose and introspective, some had the quickest and smartest brains, others were as thick as pig shit. Some of these men would give you their last penny, others were scoundrels, thieves, murderers, rapists, the lowest of society. But they were all blokes. Just blokes. And tending their lawns, pruning their rose bushes, keeping their stones clean filled Tommy with a sense of pride and honour. He knew that this was what his country did right. This was something to be proud of. None of these were forgotten, their sacrifice had not been ignored. Here they were remembered with dignity and respect within gardens that allowed them to rest easy. Beautiful, dignified places where their loved ones could visit them in comfort and in hope. Their gardens were places of light, not of gloom. Tommy had often wandered around the graves at Langemark where the Germans had been piled into, and amongst those dark oak trees and flat slabs he had felt nothing but depression and grief for his enemy. In none of the Imperial gardens had he ever felt anything but a sense of righteousness. That the right thing was being done for those that had already gone before him.

They were all perfect corners of foreign lands.

PART 4
LONDON
July 1939

Tommy shuffled back to his chair opening up the box. His legs worked slower these days and his hands were becoming gnarled and bent, but his fingers were still strong as they picked at the cardboard. He couldn't help but feel curious what it was going to look like. He knew what it would be as it had been well publicised on the radio and in the papers that everyone in the country would get them. It was just one of the signs of inevitability.

He flipped the lid back and placed his hand around the rubber that lay there. Slowly he eased the whole object out of its hold and took a good look at it. Above a great circular protrusion of a nose, two glass eyes stared back at him. He smiled, then laughed to himself. He was going to look bloody ridiculous wearing that, that was for sure. Still, it was better than the hypo helmets they had been forced to wear in the trenches, this gas mask at least looked like it would be bearable to wear. He lengthened the straps on the back of the mask, took his pipe out of his mouth and placed it gently down on the table, then he carefully eased it over his head. It wasn't going to go. He raised it again and pulled on the rubber straps again, extending them for his great cranium. This time it fit better. He wiggled it into place and took a deep breath. The smell of rubber engulfed him. It wasn't an unpleasant odour, quite comforting really in its familiarity. He pulled the mask off his head and returned it to its box. It was fine he thought to himself. He could breathe, he could see out of it, it was comfortable enough. It was fine.

Tommy picked his pipe back up and put it into his mouth, pulling on it to keep it alight. The embers glowed and he sucked in the sweet taste of tobacco. So, that was the certainty right there, he thought looking at the box. War was most definitely on its way. Again. Some said that it could be as soon as by the end of that week, most said it would be no later than the beginning of next month.

Whenever it happened, everyone should be rest assured that without doubt, gas would be used upon the innocent civilians of the country. It was an indication of the evil that was to be faced that the most heinous of weapons would be utilised.

Thus, Tommy, like everyone else had his very own personal mask.

Extraordinary, Tommy thought to himself, another war! Weren't they told that they had fought in the war to end all wars? And now, just two decades later it was happening all over again. Unbelievable! he thought. Well, it wasn't really so unbelievable. There would always be wars, it was part of the human make up. Anyhow, Tommy argued silently to himself, what had been done to the Germans at Versailles had made war absolutely inevitable. He was no lover of the Germans, but he had known it in his bones, as the conditions of that treaty became known, that by kicking the Germans down so hard was a foolish and dangerous act. Tommy, just an ordinary bloke had seen the foolishness, how, he wondered couldn't the so-called great and the good realise that by punishing a country so utterly, effectively bankrupting it in such an undignified way, that it created the perfect womb in which to nurture any evil that had a loud enough voice and bigoted enough views. That was all that had happened, he believed, some little twerp with a dodgy haircut had come along and said that he could make Germany great again. They of course believed him because they needed to believe him, and now that belief and following was leading to another war. It had been inevitable. It wasn't as if Germany had even lost the war in Tommy's mind. It had just come to an end. A ceasefire. But Germany was made to pay for everything.

Only the previous year, Tommy continued ranting to himself, hadn't Chamberlain come back from Munich, brandishing a piece of paper, telling everyone that he had guaranteed 'Peace in our time'! And now, war was a whisker away. Well, Chamberlain seemed to have got that one wrong, he thought, and wondered what the history books of the future would make of their Prime Minister. No doubt they'd deride him as a naive, deluded fool. But Tommy didn't agree. He liked Chamberlain, admired him for his belief in humanity and his determination not to accept that war was inevitable. He also knew that Chamberlain was no fool. He may have optimistically waved that piece of paper and proclaimed, "Peace in our time", he may truly have believed that peace could still be saved, but regardless, Chamberlain had assuredly bought TIME. Time to prepare. A year, so that the country wouldn't be caught off guard. Twelve precious months for the factories, the schools, the politicians, the forces to get ready, just in case. It was the most valuable commodity that Chamberlain could have come away with from Germany.

It had been clearly evident to everyone that the country was in a state of flux. Even Tommy, still in Belgium up to six months before had felt the machinations that were being made. Word filtered to all of them tending the gardens that things were changing in their home country, then rumours began to spread that they would be sent back to Britain, for their own good. In March that was what happened. Quietly and efficiently, they were all told to pack their bags and ready themselves to return home.

It was a far different country that Tommy returned to than the one he left a dozen or so years previously. It felt like it was a faster country with more motor cars, motorbikes and buses filling the London streets and the small roads and lanes outside the capital. People seemed more confident, louder, a little more brash perhaps. Maybe Tommy had just gotten too used to the quiet lanes and villages of Belgium and Northern France, the relaxed, easy going natures of his fellow gardeners and the local villagers.

Memories had cascaded over him when he unlocked his old front door and pushed it stiffly open. Twelve years does a lot to a man, it can do more to a building. The reek of damp smothered him, and his eyes were beset by a forest of opportunistic foliage that had gathered within the confines of the building, but nevertheless he could see Alice at the hearth and his boy playing at the kitchen table. Voices and laughter welcomed him and he knew that the ghosts of his past were no longer sorrowful phantoms to keep him awake at night, but joyous memories that made the old building his home once again.

He slaved at returning the house to a habitable state. He eradicated the vegetation and dealt with the rot, and whilst he worked, he observed the country to which he had returned. Even in his own semi-seclusion Tommy could see the operations that were going on around him.

Then, in the last week or so, as if following a pied piper, the children began to disappear from the city, sent to the country for safe keeping. And now, the arrival of the gas masks, they were all being given them, and they certainly hadn't been created overnight by some elves in a factory. It had all needed time, and that was exactly what Chamberlain had bought. Blitzkrieg or no, the country would be in a position to face Hitler if necessary.

Tommy looked down at his new gas mask again. He remembered the first time that gas had been used. April 22, 1915, that was the date, he knew it without fail. In the middle of the night. The date had always stayed in his head when others had dropped so easily from his memory because it was his wedding anniversary and he always found it amusing that the Germans should chose that date to use their noxious substances for the first time because Alice had always complained so much about his own loud and suffocating gas.

Tommy hadn't actually been directly affected on that date. He had been in the Ypres Salient where it was used, but he was further north and heard about it only second-hand. It was the poor French buggers down at St Juliaan that got it, well, not even proper Frenchies as he recalled, but Colonial Frenchies. Nevertheless, the poor bastards never had a clue and even less of a chance.

The story that went round the trenches was that the sentries in the French line spotted a wall of smoke drifting over from the Germans. They quickly and understandably made the assumption that it was a smokescreen behind which the Germans could hide their forces and instigate a surprise attack. Naturally the orders went out for reinforcements to join the front-line troops to help turn back the impending tide. Soon those front trenches were packed firmly with young bodies intent on fulfilling their orders. Tommy knew full well what that feeling would have been, he had felt that claustrophobia every time that he had been in the front lines before an assault over the top. Bodies packed so solidly together that even farts couldn't escape. Inevitably there was a rising sense of panic that battled with the fear of the action shortly to be engaged in. Ultimately only the escape out of the trenches quelled the fear and panic. Then, adrenalin and a sheer desire to stay alive took over and animal instincts prevailed.

Those Frenchies, Tommy knew full well would have felt that feeling of impotence against their fears, they would have felt the suffocation and the rising panic.

When that smoke reached the top of their parapets, they would all have been there, with bated breaths expecting the smoke to drift harmlessly over their heads but revealing the dark forms of their enemy in the wake. What they didn't expect was for that smoke to drop suddenly, like a stone into the bottom of their trenches. They didn't expect to be inhaling a noxious substance that made them gag and retch. They didn't expect their lungs to start to fill, or their knees to collapse beneath them, their bodies only held by the weight of numbers of their comrades. They panicked. Well of course they did. Who wouldn't? Tommy knew full well that had he been there with them he would have panicked, nothing would have stopped him from turning tail and running as far from that monstrous cloud as he could possibly go.

So, they panicked and they fled, those that could, and a breach was made in the wall of the Allies' line.

That was when fear set in all along the lines and even the men some way from St Juliaan began to panic. They all knew that if the Germans were able to break through, then they would be at Ypres in no time, the coast would be theirs by the summer and it would all be over, the war would be lost. Tommy would often reflect on that. If the Germans had just followed up that gas attack quicker and subsequently broken through the lines, how many lives would that actually have saved in the grander scheme of things?

But they didn't break through, the Germans didn't follow up

quick enough and the Canadians on the left of the French lines filled that gap. Of course they did. Canadians! The strongest, fittest, bravest men that Tommy ever met in the lines. He would swear that in all his years over there he never met a Canadian that was less than ten feet tall and not built like a brick shit house. They were legends, each and every one of them, man mountains that wouldn't let anything get in their way. And yet also polite, friendly and even brotherly. Those lads simply pulled out their handkerchiefs, unbuttoned their trousers, pissed on the cloths and stuck them over their mouths and noses. Then they filled the gap in the lines and held it. The Canadians saved the war there and then and they proved that whatever evil the Germans would try, God was with the Allies not the Boche.

Tommy often thought of that night. Of the terror that those poor colonial troops must have felt and the immensity of the actions of the Canadians — God protect anyone who dared to call Canadians colonials! Many was the day, whilst he was at Tyne Cot, that he would take himself off down to the St Juliaan Road and to the memorial that had been raised there in honour and remembrance of that night and the lives that were lost and given so bravely. It had been named Vancouver Corner and there was a magnificent plinth there with the head and shoulders of a Canadian soldier, eyes cast down on to the site where so very much had been lost and won. It was a nice walk on a good day, less than an hour from Tyne Cot. He would take some sandwiches and eat them in the shadow of that great pedestal and Tommy would picture that night in 1915. His night had been so ordinary in many ways, boring really. Their night, an historic night.

Such a vile and disgusting weapon to be used, but it wasn't a surprise to Tommy that the Germans would try anything to win the war. They would clearly stoop as low as they possibly could if they could gain an advantage. Gas! The fury that went throughout the lines when it became full knowledge that the enemy were now using gas was perhaps, for a while, the greatest weapon that the Allies had. Men who were beginning to flag in their fervour for the war effort suddenly felt their muscles tighten and their jaws clench with determination that no such abomination as the Hun would prevail in this war. That was exactly the emotion that Tommy had felt that night and for a while he would clean his gun just a bit more intently, take sentry duty with a bit more dedication to the cause and lo and behold any enemy caught near his sector and in range. The Germans were clearly a vile, unchristian beast that had to be shackled and burnt.

Tommy hadn't tasted gas that night, but he knew full well what it was like to have your lungs filled with it.

Five months later he was there at Loos, Loos-en-Gohelle where the twin tits of coal slag could still be seen despite the ravages of a year of war.

They were all told that this was the big moment, the great advance that would win them the war, and if it went really well, then they would all be in Berlin for tea-time. Fantastic! It was about time really. Tommy was beginning to tire of it all. It should all have been over by Christmas, now it was September of 1915 and it didn't really look like anything was going to change very soon.

For too long the war had become static, with little movement. The almost parallel lines were in place, Tommy on one side, Fritz on the other. Occasionally there would be a little aggressive lurch forward, then a defensive lunge backwards. The only gains seemed to be the numbers of dead being dropped into the ground. To Tommy it had often felt that there was no real desire to win the war on either side. The Germans were heavily and deeply entrenched in their lines and clearly had no thoughts about giving up their positions, but they had also seemingly lost all ambition to break through the lines of the Allies, to secure the coast, take control of the seas and better the British Empire. Perhaps the Germans had arrived at the position where they simply did not want to lose the war.

But Loos was going to change all of that. The officers told them that they were going to win the war and so it had to be true. And why were they so confident? Because they now had their very own Special Gas Companies. Well, it was only reasonable everyone argued that if the Germans could sink low enough to use gas, then so could the British. After all, they had used it first.

It was an amassing at Loos, the first time that Tommy had really felt the full scale of the British Army in France or Belgium. He wasn't aware of it then but even Rudyard Kipling's son John was amongst them; in due course it would be hard to meet anyone that didn't know that John Kipling had been at Loos.

They were all packed up into those front trenches as tightly as possible, so tightly that even the rats had no space in which to scurry. All along, on top of their lines, were the precious new weapons of the Special Gas Companies. Cylinders that would seal the fate of the Germans and send the Allies all the way to Berlin. It was a simple plan. A failsafe plan and confidence was freely emanating from the officers. The instructions and orders were clear. When the wind was blowing in the right direction… which was, towards the Germans for any of the lads that weren't sure, then the valves on the gas cylinders would be opened up, the gas would come out, blow over No Man's Land to the Germans, kill all of them over there and then the lads would just go over and spike with their bayonets any that were left breathing. Simple and straightforward. Everyone in Berlin by teatime.

They stood there with belief in their officers and butterflies in their stomachs. Tommy was in the second line to go over and his guts twisted and turned as he desperately hoped that he wouldn't throw up. It didn't matter that it was going to be an easy victory, Tommy knew full well that even if the gas killed most of the Germans, it wouldn't kill all and any that were left would be as determined to save themselves against the oncoming army as he would be in their positions. Each and every one of their guns would be facing in one direction and he was about to climb up into that direction. They felt like cattle on the way to the slaughterhouse, penned in, knowing that they were to wait for the gate to open, knowing that that gate would send them to their doom but at the same time, all eager for it to open so that they could get out of this sheer suffocation of bodies.

Tommy remembered how they all kept looking for the sign that it was on. Listening for anything, a whistle, the sounds of valves turning, an order. They were pumped both with fear and anticipation but also a primal excitement. Somewhere, someone dropped their guts. There were many stenches in the trenches and they got used to them all, but someone shitting themselves behind you or in front of you or at your side, was a toxic stench that none of them could ever prepare for. It made someone retch, someone else tried to laugh but it stuck in his throat, Tommy closed his eyes, thanked God it wasn't him that had done it and concentrated on the tiny scratches on his Lee Enfield.

The wait was becoming untenable. Some of the lads started licking their fingers and sticking them up in the air to see if they could work out which way the wind was blowing. Still nothing happened.

Then, there was a hiss. The valves were being turned and an expulsion of orange, yellow vomit was seeping from the cylinders. As one the lads looked up, curious and now keenly aware that their wait was over. Their time had come to leap through the gates and win the war. The hiss increased in intensity, the ooze that was emitted was the very essence of evil, thank God it had been the Germans that had used this first and not them. It crawled from the bowels of the cylinders and with long tentacles it grasped the land, gripped it and pulled itself towards the German lines. As Tommy witnessed the monster's release, he felt a surge of pity and despair for those that it was seeking. He had come to hate his enemy, to despise their atrocious claim of humanity, but in that moment, he felt profoundly that no-one deserved the death and torture that was being prepared by these tentacle wisps. He swallowed hard and prayed for forgiveness. Prayed for redemption. Prayed for life. The gas was allowed to make a head start towards the German lines, then the whistles began to blow, and the first line of lads climbed up the wooden ladders and out of their packed trenches. For both those leaving and those remaining for the present, it was an immediate release, all were able to grasp a little bit more air and suck it into their lungs. That first line slowly began to follow the gas across the pock marked ground that separated the two armies. The gas was their shield and their camouflage, but the Germans knew as soon as they saw the blanket of acrid smoke that the attack was on and blindly rifles and machine guns fired into the fog.

Then it was Tommy's time to climb over. He chastised himself inwardly for the shaking of his legs as he took one rung and then another up the trench wall. He desperately wanted to vomit. Every instinct within him screamed for him to flee. But he took a type of control and stepped over the parapet and brought himself erect. He held his rifle, with bayonet fixed, in front of him and slowly, as assuredly as he could make himself act, began to walk behind the first line of lads. His eyes however refused to look at those in front of him or the thinning gas that was in front of them. His gaze was fixed firmly to the ground. Pinned on his size 8 boots. Intently analysing each tread through the French soil. He was adamant in his mind that should he be destined to die today, should there be a bullet with his name carved on it, then he did not want to see it coming, he would take the bullet in perfect and sublime ignorance.

They all wanted to firmly believe in the plan and the prediction that this action would be the ending of the war. The simplicity and the faith that they put into this new great weapon fuelled their beliefs. Besides, when great men proclaimed to them that it was a faultless plan, then who were they to disagree or question otherwise. And it was a great and simple plan. Perhaps not a war ending plan, but certainly a battle winning one. Who could think otherwise? Gas the enemy and follow up by killing any that had survived. What could go wrong?

The first that Tommy knew that the wind had changed direction was the sudden chorus of screams emanating in front of him. Instantly he had to raise his head, bullets or not, he needed to bear witness. No more than twenty yards in front of him the line was in utter chaos. Tentacular fingers of putrid yellow wound like spectres around the lads who were baying like wounded hounds. Some had their hands grasping their throats or their chests, most were on their knees or their stomachs or their sides, blindly, desperately trying to escape from the monster that attacked them. Their eyes were glazing marbles racked with confusion and surprise and terror. Death was whispering in their ears and they could all hear it loud and clearly.

And then Tommy was in the fog. The wisps of death were tickling his face and hands and suddenly he was breathing in and swallowing bleach. That was what his brain was telling him. He was drinking through both his nose and mouth, bleach. Thick, viscous, burning bleach. Terror paralysed his whole body, it was as if he had stared into the eyes of a basilisk, with his feet refusing to run, to help him to escape. Instinctively he had dropped his weapon and his hands covered his face, then held desperately onto his throat, vainly hoping that they could arrest the journey of the appalling chemical. He felt his mind bursting with confusion, desperately trying to make sense of the situation, assess the damage and give him an escape route, a plan of action. But instead, there was nothing but confusion. He felt that his eyes were transfixed on the ground. They were sending him a message; it was the same message that his feet and legs were sending him. He was on solid, dry ground. And yet his brain was screaming at him in panic and terror, as his lungs were filling, that he was most definitely drowning.

Tommy would remember stumbling, a feeling of his knees buckling from fear more than anything. He would remember kneeling on the ground as if in supplication to the devil that was controlling him. Then he would remember nothing. Not the arms around his shoulders that pulled at his body. Or the slow but frantic dragging back towards his line. Or the sudden heave over the parapet and dead drop onto the trench floorboards below. He wouldn't even remember the searing pain that his brain registered as the cartilage in his nose sprayed in a hundred different directions.

He would remember occasional moments on a stretcher, being thrown around irreverently, and trench walls passing him in a blur. Sometimes a blur that struck him, sometimes as one that sailed past. He didn't remember the explosion that halted his passage through the trenches and caused his body to slide backwards and down off the stretcher as one safe pair of strong hands were lost, the head and torso of their owner in tatters. He wouldn't know the hands that picked up the fallen torch that was Tommy, or the hands that had stayed with him from the start. But he would know that they gave him a chance. That they believed in him and loved him for in that moment of rescue he, to them, was all of them. And they were the hands that they would hope and pray for.

The hands got him to the Advanced Dressing Station and dropped him amongst the increasing numbers of similarly afflicted. Then they left him and returned to where they were needed.

Periodically Tommy would rouse in a fit of coughing. His body was working in an automatic mode, reacting to the lack of oxygen, expelling the alien invader as much as it could. Blood mingled with sputum as he retched, vomited and spat. His eyes, filling with blood and pus, burned into their sockets, tears streaming in reaction, coursed like sandpaper across the orbs. And still the sensation of drowning surrounded him. He hacked and spat, convulsed and hacked again, until consciousness would drift away as the miniscule amount of oxygen delivered by the incapacitated lungs got used up in his mechanical actions.

Tommy wasn't considered an emergency case by those making the harsh decisions of who could be saved, who could wait and who didn't stand a chance. Even the caked blood over his face didn't detract their experienced eyes. There were no gaping fissures, no missing ends to his limbs. He could wait. Others were in more immediate danger.

At some point he was wetted with a damp cloth, his face

cleared of the blood, his nostrils opened to ensure something could be taken into his lungs. His eyes were wiped clean and knowledgeable hands investigated him and wrote on a small piece of brown card.

In his dreams and his waking moments, he was coughing and spluttering and trying to suck air into his lungs. In dreams the world was clearer, faces were focussed, sounds were closer. His woken eyes saw the world through a thick smoky glaze with movement being made by ill-defined shapes that were only discernible as human when they made a noise.

He would be put on stretchers, and moved into trucks and onto trains. He got sent to the coast, Boulogne, to a real hospital with proper beds and mattresses and then onto a ship bound for Shorncliffe in Kent and another hospital with young nurses who talked gently to him. He was ignorant of much of his repatriation. The gagging and heaving controlled his life, his vision remained a blur and changes in his circumstance he accepted without question.

By the time he was stretchered up the hill in Shorncliffe his coughing was abating, he could gulp at air without convulsing and shapes were recognisable forms. There was almost a jollity there in the hospital. The patients were often laughing and speaking loudly, even those hobbling around on crutches missing a leg were effervescent with the knowledge that their role in the war was over.

They both came to see him at Shorncliffe. Alice and his boy. How long they were with him he would never be able to guess for certainty. His convalescing had been going well, but he was far from being the man he once was. Tommy couldn't remember speaking to them, he wouldn't even know if he smiled. What a sight he thought, that must have been to them. What a disappointment.

He did remember that Alice sat at his side, holding his hand in hers, whilst the other brushed his face gently. Her beautiful soft voice whispered words to him that had no shape or form but were filled with love and meaning and a future. Every now and again Tommy would sense the gentle thud of a tear falling on his bed sheet, or dropping onto his face and sliding down his cheek. He knew that he had wanted to give back the comfort that he was being shown. To give a reassuring smile, a wink or a witty comment. Maybe he did. But he wouldn't know. It was just as if he had been visited in a dream where he had no effect over his actions. Perhaps that was all it had been, he wondered, a dream.

But no, he could remember clearly how his son, so much taller than when he had left him, stood proudly and erectly at the foot of his bed. He wouldn't get any closer. Wouldn't come to his father's side or take his hand. He just stood there. Almost a young man. And even in Tommy's fogged vision he could see the script written on his boy's face. It was a message of resolution and determination, of revenge. There was strength in that face and there was love and affection, but it wasn't realised in tenderness, not even perhaps kindness. It was the face of an avenging angel.

Tommy picked up the box holding the new gas mask and placed it on his knee. A tear formed, swelled and drew away from the corner of his eye. Slowly and gently, it worked its way down his cheek. That was the last time that he ever saw Alice and his boy. There in a hospital in Kent as he lay prone in his bed. It was the last time he heard her voice or felt her touch. It was the last chance he had ever had to say that he loved her and that he loved his son, and that he was proud of him and that they would all get through this and everything would be all right. He couldn't even remember them leaving. Alice standing up, kissing him goodbye or waving at him from the end of the ward. Maybe he had fallen asleep, perhaps they thought that they would leave him to his rest so that he could get better. Best not to disturb him. They'd see him again soon.

Tommy did get rest and he did get better. He got better perhaps too quickly. So quickly that he got sent back over before he could see his family again. It was a long and expensive journey to Shorncliffe for them. It had been a trip only affordable rarely in a lifetime. Once in that lifetime.

'I love you,' Tommy said out loud, not for the first time that he had spoken when alone. 'I love you and I miss you.' He knew his words were heard and understood. He had never left his family and they had never left him. But he did miss their presence.

He shook himself very deliberately.

'Pull yourself together Tommy you old woman,' he said very much to himself. 'Now you have had your fair share of gas in your lifetime, and you don't want any more do you. Put this here gas mask somewhere safe and handy so that when those bombs do start dropping it ain't going to be no worry to you.'

Tommy pulled himself up, wincing slightly at the stiffness he felt in his lower back and took the gas mask down to the front door and hung it up on one of the coat hooks that hung there. Then, without choosing a coat, he took down his cap and placed it onto his head, opened the door and stepped out into the midday sun.

PART 5
LONDON
December 1945

Without a doubt it was an extravagance and one that Tommy could barely afford, but it called out to him more powerfully than anything had for quite some time. It was a beautiful wreath and reminded him of those that Alice had made every year at Christmas. She had always made it such a special time of year, always lavishing love and festive sentiment upon her boys, propelling them both into her state of excitement and joy. Their lack of wealth meant nothing to Alice, she would make decorations and gifts for their simple home and save whatever pennies she could throughout the year to ensure that she could spoil Tommy with some extra tobacco for his pipe, perhaps an orange or some fudge, a new handkerchief or if it had been a particularly good year a goose for the table. She never asked for anything in return, but Tommy always made some effort, though he regretted now, that he had not done more. He could hardly remember what he had given her over the years, except for one, their son had been getting to the age when he would be leaving school and looking for work and Tommy had sensed a melancholy coming over Alice. It wasn't anything that she ever said, but there was a lack of laughter which was strange in their household. That year, he had bought her a simple, but pretty little locket and put two small portrait photographs in it — one of their son, and one of himself. She cried so much when she gave it to her, that he thought at first he had made a calamitous miscalculation, but that was only for a moment. She rained hugs and kisses on him that year that he would never forget, and he knew that she had understood what he was trying to say with the present. That he would always be her man, their son would always be their son, no matter where he was or how old their boy was. That was the Christmas before war broke out, the one he would never forget.

It had been a long time since he had felt any way inclined to celebrate Christmas. It wasn't because he was Scrooge-like, it was just that he couldn't find anything worth celebrating. Christmas without his Alice or his boy was just another day, or in fact worse than any other day, it was a day he just had to get through. But this year he did feel differently. He felt differently all-round. He would make an effort. He had bought a wreath and he would send out some Christmas cards, just a few, to the people that meant the most to him. His nieces of course would get cards, he might even buy them presents, well, perhaps not, he thought, maybe that was taking things a little too far, but he would most certainly send them cards!

He had been feeling more positive for quite some time. It wasn't just because the war had ended which was of course wonderful. The victory celebrations had continued throughout May after the Germans accepted defeat and then again throughout August when the Japanese were bombed into submission by the Americans. It had felt like the country was walking on air and it stayed that way for quite some time. Every returning, demobbed man and woman reminded them of the peace that had been hard fought. The stripping of the tape from the windows, the taking down of the blackout curtains, the re-emergence of signposts, the break-up of his home guard platoon, it all underlined that better days had arrived. And yet it wasn't just this that warmed Tommy's heart. He had been there in the days and months after wars had finished. When so much had been promised and optimism filled a country's soul. And he had witnessed how quickly promises are forgotten, how excuses are easily made and a normality resumes where those with the least are kept in their place. And now, in the immediate days of peace there was still plenty of hardship for all. The shops were still limited in what they could offer, and rationing wasn't going to go away any day soon. And what was going to happen to the jobs? That was anybody's guess. Would it just be as it was back when he returned from Ypres? Jobs disappearing in the armaments factories because there was no longer a need to manufacture the means of death. Would the mine owners once again take back control of their industry creating a lottery for all the miners with the sort of working conditions they could expect. Would the rents balloon again just as they had done back in the 20s crippling anyone struggling with employment? For all the nation's cloud walking, Tommy knew that the position was precarious. He knew that peace could mean backward steps and that bad times could easily be just around the corner.

But clearly Tommy had not been the only one to know. His experiences weren't isolated, they were felt deeply within the country, but he only realised that when the election results were proclaimed. That was the moment that Tommy knew he was beginning to believe again, to believe in people and a better world.

It had almost seemed inconceivable that Churchill, having won the country its peace, having held the heart and spirit of the people in fighting the evil that was Hitler's Germany together, could possibly be thrown out of office. Churchill was the saviour, it would be rude to unceremoniously dump him into the street, and rudeness was not one of the attributes most commonly given to Tommy's country. Britain was a country where everyone knew their place and politely, they would all do the right thing.

But Tommy voted against Churchill. Not because he didn't appreciate how much the great orator had done to bind the country together, but because he knew deeply that in peace time Churchill was not the leader that he wanted in his corner. In peace time he wanted a leader and a government that would hear the voices that were calling "Not Again".

Tommy couldn't believe that they had done it, that the country had acted together and made their voices heard, that they elected a government that was making wonderful, life changing promises.

Yes, yes, yes! He knew that politicians lied, that they promised one thing but did another, but this time Tommy believed. Not necessarily in the politicians, but in the country. He believed that if the promises weren't fulfilled then the country would make itself heard, would make a stand. This time, now, he felt that the country would stand together. He didn't think that they would force a civil war or anything that foolish — that sort of nonsense was for the French or the Spanish, but he did feel, no, he knew, that they would stand their ground. Make their voices heard. Go to the streets. They would proclaim, Not This Time. Enough is Enough.

They were being promised such wonderful things, crazy things, things that were unimaginable before in his lifetime.

That all the community and voluntary hospitals, the doctors and the nurses and the dentists and the opticians, would be brought together under the control of the government, and if anyone, regardless of where you came from, got the measles, or broke a leg or were going to have a baby, or had a toothache, then they could go and get treatment, a bed in a hospital, medicines and it wouldn't cost them anything, not a penny. It was an outrageous suggestion and Tommy knew it, he thought that probably the whole country knew it, he didn't really believe that it would be achieved, but it was a dream and what they all needed was something worth dreaming about.

Then they were also being promised that if they fell on bad times, were out of work or struggling to make ends meet, then the government would give them a little bit of money, not a fortune, nothing to make them rich or anything, but just enough to put a meal on the table or a roof over a head. That was a government worth having. A government that cared. A government that he, Tommy could believe in.

The new government had been in power a few weeks with Christmas looming and Tommy still felt a belief and excitement in them, in his country and now in Christmas itself. Now, after all these years he felt not so much that he wanted to enjoy Christmas, but that he was able to. That he was allowed to.

Tommy hammered a nail half-way into his front door and hung the wreath on it. It was a simple thing, a declaration to himself and anyone who passed that he believed in something better.

He remembered that last Christmas with Alice. How she loved her locket and radiated happiness. He thought about the three of them round the table laughing and singing and playing silly games. Then he remembered the last time that he had felt that essence of Christmas. It wasn't that time with his family, but the following year with almost strangers in a cold trench in France.

He had just got over there and couldn't help but feel pretty glum and downhearted about the whole situation. He had missed all the excitement, all the good stuff; Mons, the Marne, the Aisne, the Ancre and Ypres. Now all they were doing was finishing off the great lines of trenches that supposedly ran from the Belgian coast all the way down to Switzerland. Digging in and solidifying their positions. Hardly what he had hoped for, hardly the thrills that he had signed up for. And it wasn't just cold, it was absolutely freezing. They were down at Fromelles in France and the ground was frozen white, no snow, just frost and ice. It was as much as they could do to stay warm let alone make any improvements to the conditions of their trenches. On Christmas Eve he was in the Front Line. All day they devised different ways to keep themselves warm, hitting each other on the arms, doing upright press ups against the side of the trenches or jogging a few yards down their section of the trench and then back again. It was all that consumed them, the one ambition was to get warm.

Sometime before dusk, Tommy couldn't quite recall when exactly, though he knew it was still light, they heard a high-pitched voice coming in their direction down the lines on the left. What it was saying was anybody's guess, but it was clearly excited, and it was getting closer and closer. Eventually, from around the castellation of the trench appeared the originator of the noise. Younger than Tommy, but by no means a boy, his cheeks were ruddy from exertion and the cold, his mouth was spewing smoke like a dragon as he continuously repeated his phrases. He didn't pause in his running, but as he passed each man, he caught their eyes and waved his arms towards the parapet of the trench. Then he was gone, round the next corner and only evident by his gradually reducing voice.

'What the fuck was that all about?' some voice questioned.

'I dunno, I thought he was saying something about Christmas trees,' another of the lads replied.

'He said that the Germans have got Christmas trees,' said Tommy.

'Germans have got Christmas trees? He's having a laugh,' another of the cohort said from within a shallow hollow in the trench.

'Well, I'm gonna take a look,' Tommy said stepping forward from the group of men. He stepped onto the firestep and raised a periscope slowly above the lines. He cursed and brought it back down.

'Bloody thing is covered in ice,' he said and tried breathing first on the top lens and then the bottom to clear it. 'Nothing doing, I won't see fuck all out of that.' Then gingerly he stepped back up, his shoulders hunched, then slowly started to straighten up.

''Ere what you doing, you arse, you'll get your bloody head blown off, get back down 'ere', Charlie Pinner said. Charlie was built like a brick and had a reputation for never starting fights, but always finishing them. He wasn't a naturally aggressive man, but if he felt he was right in an argument, he would never let it go. He grabbed Tommy's leg and tugged at it. Tommy ignored him and raised his head fraction by fraction to the top of the parapet.

Suddenly, there was the report of a rifle firing and Tommy's cloth cap flew over the trench parados and his body tumbled backwards off the step and landed in a heap on the floorboards.

For a moment there was a stunned silence amongst the small group of men, then a soft 'shit', was uttered.

'Fuck me that was close,' Tommy muttered, his eyes opening and a broad grin creasing his face. 'I'll tell ya something though, they 'ave got Christmas trees, a whole line of them, all down their trenches. Well, not exactly Norwegian Spruce or anything, but festive twigs all right, you have to give them credit where credit is due.'

'Ere what's going on down 'ere', their sergeant appeared from round the corner not remotely appearing to be in any sort of a festive mood. 'What are those bastards shooting at? And Atkins where's your cap?'

'It's nothing sir, they must have just thought they saw something in our lines. Nothing came anywhere near us. They're just playing games that's all.' Tommy replied, ignoring the question about his cap.

'All right, well, keep your heads down. There's a double ration of rum coming down for you tonight, so you don't want to miss that.' He turned and walked back the way he came.

Tommy collapsed back onto the firestep, and took his pipe out of his tunic pocket, his hands were shaking uncontrollably with the realisation of how close he had come to meeting his maker, but a smile covered his face and he winked at the younger lads around him.

'You're a prat Tommy,' one of them said. Then a laugh went up and they relaxed.

The temperature kept dropping as afternoon gave way to evening. The stew that arrived did little to warm them, but it gave them something to do and something different to moan about. Some had covered their already gloved hands with socks, others had scarves wound round their heads leaving just small gaps where their eyes and mouths were. Tommy was fortunate, Alice had made him a balaclava that covered his neck and head, and his gloves were thick and warm. He was cold, freezing even, but not suffering as much as some of them. He looked at his colleagues, not for the first time, and considered them. Some he had known for some weeks, ever since he was sent to train with his regiment in Kent, others he had come to know very quickly. They were all younger than he was, not always by very much, but he did feel like a father figure to some degree. None of them were boys, they had all seen action in one form or another, either this time, or like Tommy in previous incarnations. In many ways Tommy could see that they were hardened men who understood hardship, understood their job and what they had signed up for. They had experiences that many hadn't, they knew the fragility of life. But he could also see the boys under those masks. Some hadn't lived a life beyond the army. This had been their way out and they had taken it, at the earliest opportunity. They didn't have wives or families, probably not even girlfriends, maybe the only girls they knew were the ones that all the lads got to know. Some of the other lads, were more like him. Their life experiences extended outside of the army, they had done their stint then lived a civilian life with families and responsibilities, only to be grabbed back as a reservist or volunteer to return to the colours out of duty or a desire to grab back their youth. In Tommy's eyes, despite the dirt and harshness of the moment and location, he saw them all as lads, on Christmas Eve, that really should have been anywhere else but there.

Above the trenches, clouds were held suspended, darkening the night from the moon and stars. Occasionally a Very light would sail over to light No Man's Land and a colourful glow would cover the freezing shapes of men huddled in twos and threes along the trench. Out of the quiet a sound broke. To begin with it was more of a noise than a sound, like an animal being trodden on. Then it became an organised sequence of notes, a tune projected from a squeezebox, and then softly voices joined in with the tune, attached themselves to it and became the song.

'What the fuck in hell is that now? Can you hear it? Fucking spooky is what it is.' Only the speaker knew who had spoken.

'It's the Germans,' a voice replied. 'They're singing ain't they. Christmas carols I think.'

'That ain't Christmas carols,' another voice contradicted. 'They've got all the words wrong.'

'Well, they may 'ave all the words wrong, but it's the right melody, that's Silent Night that is.'

The German voices were slowly increasing in volume as more joined in. The singing was the reaching of humanity from one line to the other and it became infectious. Some of the men began to hum along, and then they added their own words.

'Screw that,' the distinctive voice of the sergeant yelled out, 'if we're going to sing Christmas songs, we ain't going to sing German fucking Christmas songs.' And in a loud baritone he began to belt out O Come All Ye Faithful.

It was as if the whole line was looking for a choirmaster as a cavalcade of voices merged with the sergeant's. Whether it was the notion of festive will or a competitive streak to outdo the musical attempts of the enemy it was hard to discern. But it was contagious, and it continued song after song, hour after hour. Sometimes the Germans seemed to be in the energy ascendancy, sometimes it was the British. Somewhere, in one of the lines a violin was brought into the mix, someone else found a harmonica.

To an outsider caught in the middle between the two choirs they would have heard a chaotic melange of notes, voices and words, but if they were to edge closer to any one line, they would have picked up a passion that wasn't just about outdoing an enemy, but also about individual lives and desires. The melodies and words may have differed, but the sentiments were matched. The hours passed and as promised by the sergeant extra rations of rum came down the lines which invigorated any that felt their passions draining.

Inevitably, sometime before dawn, the singing faded and eventually stopped. And then the orders came for Stand To and the lads shook themselves together and stepped up onto the firestep, rifles in hand and aimed over towards their enemy. All eyes desperately trying to focus on the parapets ahead of them, to judge if there was any movement, any indication that an attack would be attempted on this, the most holy and inappropriate of days. Many of them felt that if the Germans were to mount an attack on any day, because of all the stories they had heard of them, this would actually be the day.

It was clear after a while that nothing was being prepared against them, so the orders came to Stand Down and the usual mess of actions ensued. Some immediately collapsed into a heap, desperate for some sleep, others began to clean their rifles, whilst breakfast was on the minds of some.

Tommy wasn't sure what exactly it was, but something had gotten into his mind. It may have been the long night, the cold, the rum, or even perhaps the Christmas spirit. Whatever it was he didn't know at the time and he would never know afterwards, but he felt that his actions weren't being wholly governed by himself. He took a handkerchief from his pack and tied it securely around the top of his Lee Enfield. Then slowly, carefully, he raised it high above his head and began to wave it left to right. Then he stood up on the firestep and took hold of a rung of one of the ladders leaning there, then he levered himself onto the first rung. He arched his head and shoulders backwards as far as he could so that his face was almost parallel to the top of the parapet. Then, with his lips almost showing to any beady eyed German, he wet them, took a deep breath and shouted out:

'Hap—py Christ-mas Friiiittttzzzzz!'

Tommy waited for a response. There was nothing. Not a sound came back at him. Not even the report of a rifle telling him to fuck off. So, he tried again, louder, more insistently.

'Hap—py Christ-mas Frrrriiiiiiiiiitttttttttzzzzzzz!' Again, he waited, and then suddenly, the reply came.

'Hap—py Christ-mas Tommy.'

With that, Tommy almost fell off the rung in astonishment. How the bloody hell did they know his name?

Then he gathered himself back together and took a firm hold of the ladder. With the rifle still high in the air above him and waving slowly side to side, he stepped onto the next rung. And then the next.

'What the fucking hell are you doing you twat? You'll get your fucking head blown off. Get back down here.' A strong grip held Tommy's calf and prevented him from moving. Tommy looked down. It was Jack Gooding, one of the old sweats that he had come over with. Tommy smiled down and winked.

'Trust me, Jack. I'll be all right'.

On his other side Tommy felt the butt of a rifle press into the cheek of his arse. 'Up you go there, Tommy, go and see your mates!'

Tommy looked at the provoker, smiled and winked, then turned his head to the sandbags lying in front of him. His eyes were now above the top and he gave any half decent sniper a clear shot. He looked over the empty space between the two lines to the German sandbags. A long line of black spikes, the top of the pickelhaubes, stretched in front of him. Then slowly the helmets seemed to levitate, and he could see a line of white foreheads beneath the spikes, then eyes, and noses and full faces. He pushed himself up onto the next rung and then the next and as he emerged from his trench the Germans in front of him were mirroring his actions. His stomach churned with nervousness and excitement. He felt that he was either doing an incredibly brave and good thing or a terribly disastrous one. Whichever, it was ridiculously dangerous. But there was something in the air, something was inside of him taking a control of his actions.

Tommy stretched further and then lowering his aching arm for a moment, he placed the butt of his rifle onto the top of the parapet to act as a crutch to get himself completely out. Then he righted his back, stood upright and raised his head. Suddenly the bravado and confidence that he had felt up to that point washed out of him like a plug being lifted and his legs felt their sturdiness disappear. In front of him, perhaps just a hundred yards away was a line of towering German soldiers, for all he knew in that moment it could have been the whole of the German Army and they were walking slowly, but steadily, towards him. He felt an almighty lump thrust itself into his gullet and involuntarily he gasped for breath. He realised that he hadn't quite thought through his plan, if he had ever had anything in his head that could constitute a plan. He desperately wanted to step forward, but panic was tearing through him and he was glued to the spot. But then he became aware of movement, turmoil even, around him, by his feet. He looked down. A hand was gripping to the ground, then an arm appeared, a face, shoulders and a whole body. His eyes raised their focus slightly, dozens of limbs were hoisting bodies to the top of the trenches. He turned his head, and the same thing was happening on the other side. Then by his sides, in a long and increasing line the lads had joined him and looked to him for a lead.

Buoyed with renewed confidence, Tommy set a leg forward towards the Germans, their hated enemy. The lads copied his action, and two parallel lines of soldiers began to converge on one another.

As the space between them diminished, hands began to stretch out in over emphasised greeting, some called a welcoming hello, some waved. Both lines illustrated a nervousness in their actions but also a clear and decisive movement that their actions were warranted and legitimate. When they were within about ten feet of each other, without an order being uttered, both lines came to an abrupt halt as if reason had been suddenly made. Eyes met eyes, and uncertainty, for a moment seemed to prevail. Both sides were seeking assurances and leadership.

Tommy delved his hand into his pocket and pulled out a partially eaten bar of chocolate, then ostentatiously proffered it to the lad standing most directly opposite him. The effect was instantaneous. Other hands began searching in pockets for treasures that could be shared. Smiles, laughs and greetings erupted amongst the men and two lines of soldiers became one line of men. Hands were shaken forcibly and intently, shoulders were patted heartily, chocolate bars were broken in two, cigarettes were liberally thrust into hands. The actions were of universal generosity and friendship. Some would find pictures of their families back home to share, others found bottles of wine or tots of rum, jars of marmalade, tins of tobacco. It was a moment when the war had ceased to exist. Nationalities became an irrelevance. The true differences between men became evident to them all, it didn't exist.

The German with whom Tommy shared his chocolate was a good six inches taller than him, he had a hefty moustache and eyes that sparkled with laughter. He chewed the chocolate without breaking his smile, then in return offered Tommy an orange. Tommy could scarcely believe it, an orange? Here in the middle of nowhere. How on earth did he get that? It wasn't perhaps the healthiest orange that he had ever seen, but the thought of tasting it made Tommy's mouth water. He smiled and nodded his head enthusiastically. The German dug a dirty thumb nail into the top of the piece of fruit and scored a line down the peel. Deftly he picked at the tear and pulled away the skin to reveal the juicy segments underneath. When it was disrobed, he pulled it in two and gave one half to the Englishman.

'Thank you,' Tommy automatically responded and took the segments. 'Danke schon'.

'My pleasure Englishman, enjoy.'

Tommy sucked on the fruit, savouring the sweet juice. It was a taste of home. A taste of Christmas and for a moment he was back in his front room with the fire lit, in the arms of his family. It was the pure, dainty fingers of Alice that had peeled the orange for him, an orange that she had picked especially for its firmness, its size, its purity and succulence. The soft, puckered fruit that Tommy was finishing off would have fared poorly in comparison to any orange that Alice had chosen for him, but in that moment, it tasted better than any he had ever eaten in his life. He looked into the eyes of the grinning giant in front of him and wondered if his mind was being read.

'You like it?' The German questioned.

'It is the best orange I have ever tasted in my life, thank you.'

'Pah,' retorted the German. 'It is a poor example of a fruit, but I have saved it for today, and I am pleased that you have enjoyed it.'

'Your English is very good,' replied Tommy.

'Of course! Before all this nonsense started, I worked for many years as a waiter in England. In Brighton. I have had plenty of practice.'

'Brighton?' questioned Tommy. 'Where in Brighton? I know it well; I often took my family there.'

'Indeed! I worked mostly at The Palace Hotel, but also some other smaller restaurants.'

'The Palace? We often went there. You could have served us!'

'Yes, my friend, I could. But no longer, eh? Now we are different. Now we are enemies. Now we must kill each other.'

Tommy looked into the German's eyes, not sure whether he was joking or being serious. The smile and laugh had been replaced by a sadness in his eyes. Then, as if pulling himself together he laughed.

'But not today eh! Today is Christmas. Today we are all friends. Tell me, have you got a picture of your family? I have one of mine. I'll show you.'

Tommy didn't know how long he spent in the German's company. It would feel just like a few minutes, but it was probably more like hours. They chatted, questioned each other, talked about their families and shared whatever they had about them that was worth sharing. It felt to Tommy like an ordinary Sunday afternoon back home, out on a walk in the park, meeting an old pal on the way to the pub.

All around him the same thing was happening. Little groups were clustered together intently interested in each other. Some resumed their singing of the night before, forming spontaneous choirs. Others seemed engrossed in serious conversation and discussion whilst some were laughing, teasing and sharing jokes.

Inevitably the language being spoken was English but occasionally there were stalwart attempts at a pidgin German, or French became the universal communicator. Regardless of the words spoken, the sentiment that abounded was the same.

Humanity.

Tommy savoured every moment knowing that he was experiencing something unusual and very special, subconsciously he stored away, deep into his memory banks, every scene that his eyes took in, every word spoken, every morsel of food or drink shared and the features of every face that he talked to that day.

Tommy would later learn that there were similar experiences all down the lines, but his day was personal, he had instigated it and he owned it, nothing would ever take that away from him.

In other places it would be later said that religion brought men together, a Christian calling that compelled men out of their ditches to meet their enemy and come together in prayer. That wasn't how it was for Tommy, and he saw little supplication to a deity going on, for him it was simply a moment of spontaneity that he had grasped, nothing more or less.

It was even largely reported that a football match was played somewhere down the lines, Germany versus England, victors to take home all the spoils.

Nonsense, Tommy thought when he first read it in a newspaper, utter fairy-tale nonsense. The papers needed stories for their readers, so they created them, mythologised the facts in order to take ownership for their own agendas, their own propaganda. Like the Angels of Mons. Fables created to make the whole military cause meaningful. It made it a certainty that if God had sent angels to Mons then the war that the country was engaged in had to be just, and God was on the side of the righteous, Britain.

It was all garbage and Tommy detested it. He inherently hated the newspaper stories and deplored the attempts to make simple truths into what they were not. The fraternisation, which is what it became known as. Fraternisation, Tommy would always spit out the word in disgust, had nothing to do with religion, sport, politics or of good against evil, it was simply about blokes being blokes. On that Christmas Day when so comparatively few of them had really engaged the enemy mano a mano, had really felt the harsh grotesqueness of battle and war, and had not experienced the deprivations that men could sink to when life became a meaningless mire, then the overpowering emotion was for them all to put their differences aside, see reason and be human, be blokes.

Tommy had known before that the other stories that he and all of them had read weren't true. The tales of butchery and of babies being eaten by the soldiers as the German Army ploughed their way through the lowlands of Belgium. They were simply literary devices to provoke reason to hate.

In truth Tommy had been disappointed that it was the Germans that brought him back into khaki, he had never foreseen them as an enemy of his country, it was the French that he had wanted to fight. Surely the French were the natural enemy, not the Germans, hadn't the Prussians fought with them to defeat Napoleon at Waterloo? That epoch defining victory that every young English boy wanted to emulate when they grew up.

In those festive hours on the hardened soil in France amongst unsegregated men Tommy knew the lies for what they were and knew that he, just like all of them, had been caught up in the jingoistic trap and become pawns for those with the agendas. These men with their dark uniforms and spiked helmets weren't any different to the lads he was sharing trenches with. They may have been bigger on the whole and spoke with ridiculous accents, but otherwise they were just blokes, just like him. Ordinary blokes out for the day.

He wouldn't remember what the impetus was, but gradually the men began to filter back into their trenches. He would later surmise that most likely it was the calling of their bellies for better sustenance than some boiled sweets and stale wine. Hands were shaken again, and backs were patted in parting, and the armies resumed their rightful places albeit with a certain reluctance.

Tommy had been the first out and he was going to be one of the last to climb back into the trenches. He clung to the moments, instinctively realising that once he gave them up, they would be gone forever. With the darkness approaching however, and the chill of night beginning to bite, he pulled his great coat closer to him and started towards his lines.

'Tommy! Hey, Tommy, wait up.' A voice called to him from the German lines.

Blimey, Tommy thought to himself, everyone knows my name, I must have made some sort of impression if nothing else. He looked up trying to gauge where the voice was coming from. He didn't need to be a detective. From twenty or so yards away a tall, lanky figure was waving wildly at him.

'Tommy, Tommy, wait, stop,' the figure repeated.

Tommy stopped and watched the figure, curious and suddenly a little nervous. It was monstrously tall and now it was loping over to him like some great giraffe, arms pounding the air in desperation to make haste.

The figure got to Tommy and immediately wrapped his arms tightly around him. Then he kissed him, strongly with intent, first on the right cheek and then on the left. Tommy's spine chilled and he would always later recall that he was never more scared during that war than he was in that moment being embraced by a German.

Then the German stepped back slightly and took Tommy's hand in his. With his other hand he fished in his trouser pocket. Not revealing to Tommy what it was, he unfurled Tommy's fingers, placed something in his palm and wrapped his fingers back up, taking the fist in his own hand. He looked deeply and earnestly into Tommy's eyes.

'Happy Christmas Tommy. May God be with us all.'

Then, without saying another word or offering another look, the German turned and headed back into the darkening afternoon to his lines.

Tommy uncurled his fingers. There was a simple, thin, silver chain resting in his palm, attached to the chain was a small Star of David. He looked up again to try and see the German, but he was already gone. Tommy would never know the name of the man or what became of him, but he would never forget his face and that star on its chain would never leave him from that moment onwards. It would always be carried in his trouser pocket, placed in his shoe at night when he slept, or in later years on the table by his bed. For all the luck that he was blessed with in his life, Tommy would always consider the star as being responsible.

Tommy subconsciously fondled the necklace that lay in his pocket as he pictured that special day and in particular the face of that German. He knew that that Christmas Day had been the last time that he had truly felt hope and faith in the human spirit. He remembered thinking, as he climbed back down into the trenches to join the lads that everything had changed. He had changed. The whole mood of the line had altered. There was a quiet thoughtfulness within the trenches.

As tea was brewed men talked softly to each other, they sat pensively, much of the aggressive bravado against their enemy had disappeared.

In Tommy's head during those minutes, he couldn't imagine that the war could now possibly continue. Now that they had met their enemy and broken bread with them, there was no way that they could fire at them, attempt to kill them. They had seen that the subversive propaganda against the Germans was just that, a device to instil hatred where there was no reason for it. Tommy felt a humanity filling him, a genuine warm glow that he was a better man than he had previously supposed, they were all better men. Deep in the trenches there was a filial love that he had never imagined existed. As he sat there on Christmas Day 1914 supping at a cup of diesel infused tea, Tommy believed in all of them, irrespective of their places of birth. He trusted that they could look out for each other and could make the world a better place. He knew in those moments that this wasn't a naivety, this was a possibility, he had seen and been part of the possibility, and witnessed that it existed in the world.

Sat alone, so many years later, he brought out that Star of David from his pocket and examined it. He knew it so well. For all its tiny size, he could describe every contour, every nick in its surface. This Star had become as much a part of him as his fingers, legs and his nose. He knew, looking at it that a few months after receiving it, probably by the end of February of the following year, certainly by the middle of March, if he had seen a German, he wouldn't have hesitated in skewering him with his bayonet. He wouldn't have hesitated, and he wouldn't have thought twice afterwards. But back in that trench, on Christmas Day he had most definitely been a different person, a better person, with beliefs and hopes that could be realised.

Thirty odd years later in the warmth of his home, the fire crackling, his pipe lit and a mug of tea by his side, those beliefs were returning. He glanced over at the newspaper that he had thrown onto the table earlier that morning. The headlines were marketing hope. Attlee and Bevan were extolling virtues of government and people, that might just be possible. Change was perhaps finally inevitable.

He stood up and went to the great oak dresser that stood in the corner of the room and switched his Bakelite radio on. It crackled and then spluttered into a semblance of life, gradually getting louder as the valves warmed up. Music began to swim through the room, the voice of Bing Crosby, of course it was. Let it snow, let it snow, let it snow.

Tommy sat back down and tilted his head backwards as if that helped his thinking process. So long, so very long since he had believed. Thirty years. Thirty-one years. But he did believe. He did, he could feel firmly inside him, that he had belief. In humanity. In people. Changes could be made. The world could be a different place. People could look after each other. This was the moment. This was the time. And he knew suddenly that he was of that time. He smiled. Not a half-raise of the lips smile in recognition of a nice fact, but a full smile that showed his teeth; those that he had left, and lit up his eyes. He smiled and he chuckled.

Then he could see Alice and his boy, a Christmas so long ago, his son only five or six, playing on the rug in front of the fire. He had a wooden train engine that he was rolling along the rug, first to the left and then to the right, and as he did so he made chuffing noises as he imitated the engines that Tommy had taken him to see so many times.

'I love you,' Tommy said out loud and it was as if his son turned his head away from the train for a moment and looked up at his father and smiled. Then he returned his attention to his toy.

Tommy closed his eyes and felt the fingers of Alice running through his hair, stroking his head then brushing his cheek.

'Another tea, love?' He could hear her ask. 'I love you Alice,' he said.

'I love you too my love.' He could hear her reply as clear as Bing Crosby on the radio.

His eyes glistened with half-formed tears, then he smiled and opened his eyes. The fire crackled, full of life. No-one played on the rug and there were no fingers in his hair. And yet, his home was full of warmth. He sat alone but he was surrounded by love. His family were still, after all the years, imprinted on the tableau of his life. They were as much with him now as then.

Then suddenly he stood up.

'Right,' he said out loud. 'That's enough now Tommy.'

He went to the fire and poked it down, spreading the embers of the logs, dampening down the flames. Then he stepped over to the radio and turned it off, walked out of the room and closed the door behind him to keep as much warmth in as possible. Then he went to the coat pegs that were on the wall by his front door, took down a scarf and wrapped it round his neck and grabbed his overcoat and put it on, instinctively fastening it tightly round his body. Finally, he picked his cap off from a peg and placed it on his head, opened the door and stepped out into the brisk but bright day.

Anyone that didn't know him that passed him by that morning would have seen an old man trundling down the road. But in his mind, he was far from old. His legs and back might ache a little more than they used to and maybe he didn't walk as fast, but his mind hadn't changed and that was all that really mattered. To Tommy he was very little different to how he had always been. Certainly, on this day, he felt no different than how he had done thirty-one years ago.

He first stopped off at the grocers at the end of his road. A small, family run business that he had known so very well for much of his life. Tommy had known the grandfather of the lad that owned it now, but it was his young teenage son that helped him pick out the eight choicest oranges that they had, popping them into two brown paper bags. Tommy paid him and wished him a Happy Christmas. He almost felt like Scrooge on Christmas Day, the way his heart was full and warm.

He could have walked the rest of the way, but he knew he would probably have to walk back, so he saved his limbs and caught the bus that took him into town, and then another that took him to the other side of town. It wasn't much of a walk from there, and Tommy was pleased of it. Generally, he preferred walking wherever he went, sat in a crowded bus that hiccupped along would tend to make him frustrated and irritable.

It wasn't that they particularly lived on the better side of town, but it was certainly a nice road. The houses were all privately owned, and they had low brick walls in front of them rather than the usual hedges or picket fences.

The gate squeaked noisily as he opened it and he thought that maybe it would be nice if he came back and oiled it some other day. It would be no bother, he could just do it the next time he was in the area. Wouldn't even have to mention it.

He strode up the path and stepped into the porch, took the small brass knocker and rapped it three times strongly on the door. Then he stood back and waited. He heard a door open followed by quick steps coming towards him. A key turned and the door was flung open.

'Uncle Tommy, what a lovely surprise, come in, come in.' It was still a beautiful face, not quite forty, of an alabaster complexion. The smile was full and radiant and the hands that stretched out in welcome to Tommy were graced with long dainty fingers. 'So lovely to see you, we weren't expecting you. Joan will be here shortly, she'll be thrilled to see you. Come in, come in, let me take your things.'

Even had he not wanted to, there would have been no choice but to do as he was told. The woman's actions were quick and decisive as if ensuring that no alternative could be made but her wishes.

As Tommy unbelted his coat and unwound his scarf he looked at his niece. There was so much about her that resonated of Alice. He hadn't really noticed it before, or perhaps subconsciously he had, but some act of self-protection had kept it from him.

'Thank you my darling, I just thought I'd pop over. I was going to get you a card, but then thought I'd bring you a small gift. Nothing much you understand.'

'Oh, don't be so silly, there's no need for anything like that, it's just so very wonderful to see you Uncle. And look, here's Joan.'

As if in response the gate creaked. 'Look Joan, it's Uncle Tommy.'

Tommy turned to greet his other niece who was almost skipping up the path in excitement, leaving her husband to click shut the gate. Wordlessly she threw her arms about his neck and kissed him enthusiastically on the cheek.

'Uncle Tommy this is wonderful, what a fabulous surprise.' Joan squeaked almost as loudly as the gate between the kisses she was planting on her uncle's cheek.

'Right, everyone in then,' Joan's sister ordered, and they dutifully stepped inside. Joan's husband, bringing up the rear, placed his hand on Tommy's shoulder.

'Good to see you Tommy, it's been a long time. I think you've just made their Christmas.' Tommy turned to look at the younger man and simply smiled.

They were all ushered into the front room where two boys were playing cards with their father on a dark wood dining table.

'Look everyone, Uncle Tommy has come to visit, how wonderful is that!' the woman proclaimed to her family as if they couldn't possibly have realised from the commotion at the front door what was going on.

All three turned and welcomed their special visitor in as if he wasn't a stranger.

'I just wanted to come and wish you Happy Christmas that's all,' Tommy said. 'And give you a small gift.' He opened up the bags and one by one took out an orange, first giving one each to his nieces, then his grand-nephews and then to the two husbands.

'Uncle, that's lovely, thank you, but you didn't have to do that,' said his niece.

'Dolly,' Tommy said, turning back to his niece. 'I want you to go and put the kettle on, then I want you all to sit with me. I want to tell you about these oranges.'

'Of course, Uncle, of course, tea all round it is.' Dolly replied and with a huge smile fastened onto her face she turned and left the room to go to the kitchen.

PART 6
LONDON
1956

Tommy had a good life, and he knew it. It wasn't filled with material wealth, but that was of no consequence, that sort of wealth was something he had never put any value to. What his life was filled with was contentment. He was happy.

Much of that success was because of his family, his nieces in particular. He hadn't missed a Christmas with them since 1945 and each week one or sometimes both of them would pop in to see him with an offering of some stew or a pie or a fruit cake that they had made. They would always stay and fuss over him for a while, do a bit of cleaning, iron his clothes or do some of his laundry. They showed Tommy uninhibited love and he cherished them for it. He would inevitably greet them with a gruff 'I haven't croaked yet', but it was only for show, he looked forward to seeing them and loved them as much as if they had been his own daughters.

It was an easy life, an existence that he enjoyed and was proud of. He knew it might not be the excitement filled life that many would seek, perhaps not the life he would have been content with in years gone by, but he was older now and what he savoured was a nice regular schedule, with few dramas, some laughs and his family and friends. That was what he had, and he was thankful every morning for his good fortune.

He no longer sprung out of bed in the mornings like he once had. Most days he didn't wake until gone eight, which would have been unthinkable even a few short years before. Waking up though wasn't the immediate precursor to getting up. His limbs were slow nowadays, stiff and a little painful. They took time to warm up and offer his body the assistance it needed to stumble downstairs to his toilet — an inside one of which he was quite proud. His ankle was a hindrance as well at the moment, not so much an age issue as a clumsiness that had resulted in some hospital time. Nevertheless, he could still make his way downstairs in the morning without too much of a problem and he could still look after himself as he had done for much of his life.

Most mornings he would pop a 78 onto his gramophone player, usually something jolly of the ilk of Al Jolson or Benny Goodman, nothing like the noise that the young ones were inflicting on everyone these days. Then whilst it was playing, he would boil an egg or grill some bacon, make a brew and toast some bread. Then he would sit in his armchair, with the other side of the record playing, or perhaps a different record altogether and enjoy his morning slowly with the newspaper folded in half so that he could hold it with one hand. Every Monday, regardless of the weather, Tommy would take himself down to the Post Office always aiming to be there just before midday to avoid any queuing and before it shut for dinner. His pension was a marvel to him every week. The fact that he was given money just for being old. How great was that! His grandfather or father never got money for being old, but he did, that was the type of country he lived in now. A country that cared and looked after its own. The rest of Monday was pretty much taken up with the efforts of simply returning home. Where once he would have done the trip easily and quickly it was now more time consuming, but it didn't worry him, it was just the way it was, and he felt privileged that he had been blessed by still being around to do it. He could of course have caught the bus, there was one that stopped practically right outside his house, but as long as he could walk, he would walk. Once the bus became a regular feature of his life, he knew he was on the slippery path to infirmity.

Then Tuesday was his day out with the lads.

Harry was Tommy's closest friend now and lived in the same street, three doors down. They had met by chance one morning in the bookmakers. They got chatting about the races at Epsom that day on which they were both planning to place their bets and found that they had more in common than simply horseracing. Tommy always felt that when he shook the hand of Harry on that first occasion, when he barely knew him, just introducing himself, he felt an energy between them. He would chide himself with its fancifulness, but he always thought that it was like shaking hands with a brother, someone that he had known all his life.

Tommy didn't really know Harry's wife, not properly, she had always been the one kept indoors and at most would wave from an upper window when they were leaving. But she always seemed, to Tommy, to be shouting at Harry. As soon as he knocked on the door, he would hear a great shrill bellow erupt from the depths of their home calling her husband's name. She would never deign to open the door to Tommy herself and he could never decide whether her shouting was done in anger, irritation or because Harry was deaf. Harry never seemed particularly deaf to him, but then maybe neither of them heard what the other said properly.

Once Harry had been collected, they'd both head off into the town to One-Eyed Jack's. Jack had just the one eye, which was what led to the nickname. Neither of them had known him when he was better endowed and the story that he gave was that he had lost half his sight when working as a stoker on the railways. He would always claim that a piece of burning coal was spat out of the firebox one time and struck him directly in the eye. Depending on the audience or the number of pints he had downed, the story could be a gore fest of sizzling flesh with his eye exploding like popcorn, or a simple 'hurt like fucking hell'. Regardless, Jack had worn a patch ever since. But he hadn't lost his job and kept working on the lines until he was eventually told that he was too old and had to stop. He hadn't taken the news well at the time and continued to moan about his lack of employment every Tuesday when with Tommy and Harry. Jack didn't have a wife to shout at him, she had died of cancer the same year that he lost his job, but he had a daughter with whom he lived and who loved him with the patience and adoration that only a daughter can.

Tommy, Harry and One-Eyed Jack, three aging musketeers in their own imaginations, would habitually make their way to a pre-ordained cafe or hotel, or even sometimes the club. There they would enjoy each other's company over a hot meal and a pint. Often their voices would be raised in debate over the state of the world and the politicians that tried to run it. There were none that could organise the country as well as they surely could if given half the chance. Then, with the inevitable second pint half-finished in their hands the playing cards would be brought out, shuffled and dealt and the rest of the afternoon would succumb to the quiet, careful playing of whist, or even sometimes rummy.

Wednesday through to Friday Tommy considered as his working week. There were a few local widows who would ask him to clean their windows or for help putting a shelf up, cutting their lawns or doing some decorating. And every Friday he would head to his nieces' side of town where there was a fella with a bob or two that liked him to clean his motor car. He didn't take on anything too strenuous and he always took the greatest of care to do the best job that he was capable of. Tommy didn't do it for the money, although the extra pennies afforded some little niceties now and again, an extra pint or two on Saturdays, a visit to the cinema, a fresh cream cake, a bunch of flowers for his nieces. Tommy worked for his own sanity and self-worth, and to remain social, a part of his community.

Then there was Saturday. Saturday was the best day of the week. Saturday was the day that he always looked forward to, it was the one day that he always visited the club.

If there was one thing that Haig had done right in Tommy's mind it was the British Legion. He didn't necessarily think that Haig had only done one thing right, doubtlessly he had done many things right, it was just that nowadays Haig had plenty of detractors and Tommy didn't always know which side he himself came down on. He agreed with some things that were written and said, didn't know one way or the other about other things, and sometimes felt very disinclined to agree with other things. But, when it came to the club, there was no doubt in his mind, and he would back Haig on it until his dying breath. The British Legion was theirs and it would always be theirs, it was a community and a home. It was a badge that they could wear with honour. The club was his other family. And every Saturday night Tommy was down there, pushing open the front door just after seven to go and take his place up at the front room bar. He had his seat. It was unquestionably his, always waiting for him to take ownership. His drink, a pint of pale ale, would be placed in front of him within moments accompanied by a smile, a welcome and an enquiry about his state of well-being. Some would have already arrived before him; some would turn up later. On some rare occasions, when his wife allowed him, Harry would turn up too. One-Eyed Jack never felt an affinity with the place. But to Tommy it was a great part of his life.

There were still plenty that turned up who, just like him, had been subject to Haig's orders, but there were also now the children of his generation and even some of their children that came. But the younger generations didn't come into the front bar, or if they did, through some accidental opening of the wrong door, or lack of knowledge of etiquette, they didn't remain long. It wasn't a rule that they weren't allowed, it wasn't an aggressive forcing of non-integration, it was just an unspoken understanding that the front bar was the haven of the first line. It wasn't a hierarchical thing, there was no class distinction between when they had served, or even if they had served. It was just the way that it had evolved. The front bar was sacred.

The main room with the stage, that was for the younger ones, the families who brought their children and played bingo or open the box, who danced to the god-awful music that Tommy detested played by kids who were barely out of nappies.

Rock and Stroll he thought they called the racket. He hated it and couldn't understand why it was let into the club. Someone had told him that it was to ensure the club would keep attracting younger members, so that it wouldn't die out like the dinosaurs. Well, in Tommy's mind, as long as the beer was as cheap as it was it would never die out, but if it took that insult to his ears to keep it going, then he felt they would all be better off without it.

Yet he still came every Saturday and found his spot. Drank his beer and waited for the music to end. That was the real moment that he craved, the moment that he spent his week looking forward to. When the band would stop, and the youngsters would start filtering home and the whole of the club would be truly theirs for an hour or so.

For a few minutes the only noise would be chatter. The normal hubbub of noise that could have been in any pub or working man's club on a Saturday night. Then there would be the soft bump of wood hitting wood as someone lifted up the lid of the beer besmirched piano and pushed it back. The legs of the piano stool would scrape against the wooden floor and then it would creak with complaint at the heavy backside falling onto it. Finally, a dull thud of a half-filled glass being placed on the top of the instrument.

And then, the moment. A theatrical spray of arpeggiated notes from low to high followed by an eight fingered solid chord.

It was the signal that they had all been waiting for, the whistle blown before going over the top. As a company they would leave their seats or conversations and converge on the piano and its player. A wispy haired, bespectacled, moth-eaten company that became once again what they had been so many, many years before.

The player never had to be particularly good. Rarely was anyone ever very good. But they always knew a few chords and how to stride them on the piano, and a multitude of songs that could be squeezed around those chords.

Every Saturday, around that piano, Tommy was back with the lads and to the old days. The old days. Not the Good Old Days, because they weren't good old days, they were bloody awful days. But occasionally in those days there had been good times, and often as not it would have been around a piano that the good times would have been had. It could have been at an estaminet or a cafe or Talbot House in Poperinge, it didn't matter where, the moments were the same. The piano would play, and the lads would sing and nothing else mattered.

Now they sang the same songs. The songs that they all knew and would never forget, of the Mademoiselle from Armentiere who was the hardest working girl in town but did her living upside down, that would do it for wine and rum and sometimes chewing gum, who won the Croix de Guerre for washing soldiers' underwear. They would sing of Tipperary, but of course not of Tipperary, to the lads, Tipperary became Mary. It wouldn't be a long way to Tipperary, but the wrong way to tickle Mary, the wrong way to kiss. The songs were their songs. Their possessions. Only they knew their words. The sacred words. Not the sanitised lyrics that wives and girlfriends sang, but the real words that had evolved spontaneously in dugouts, camps and on marches amongst lads walking towards or from their impending doom.

There was hardly ever any talking around the piano, no recollecting of similar incidents or recounting of experiences. They all had their own stories of course, as everyone does, but this was never the time nor the place. For some of them there was never a time or a place to bring back the sights and sounds of that time. They had not uttered a word about their lives back then since even returning over the Channel, not even to their closest ones, or particularly not to their closest ones. The scenes that they had been witness to, the actions that they had participated in, the desecration of humanity was something that they wished to bury forever deep into their subconscious, never to be delved for, never to be returned to the top of their minds. Only the music was allowed.

Others would happily talk about their wars. Tommy was one of them. His war was one that he could touch at any time, freely and without risk. Feel it, sense it and bring it into the foreground of his mind accepting it simply as experiences that he shared and lived through. His war was a sequence of scenes, some of which he was proud of, some of which just existed and some of which he was ashamed of, but they were nothing more than scenes. They didn't now define him as an individual, they had just been a part of his life and he would talk to anyone about them.

Some wanted to hear about the worst things, the death and the mud and the bodies on the barbed wire, others wanted to hear that it had all been worth it, and then occasionally there would be those who would want a light-hearted tale to know that it had not all been a time of darkness and desolation. In the same sentence that he could bring a listener to tears about his war, he could bring a peel of laughter. Tommy was a natural storyteller and he wasn't alone. Many of the lads didn't hide the images of their past from their minds. For these lads their stories were inevitably the exorcising of their ghosts.

But around the piano on Saturday nights the ghosts weren't exorcised. The ghosts were not acknowledged.

Then there were also those men who had such little to tell of their war. Through no fault of their own the moments of history had passed them by and they hadn't even been spectators let alone participants. The war to these lads were days of abject boredom, mindless parading and drilling, tons of laundry or gallons and gallons of stew preparation. Even to some of those that had actually tasted the bitter tang of the front lines the stories that they could tell were of scant interest or drama for the grandchildren that would sit on their knee begging for a tale of the Great War. One lad, Tommy didn't know his name, though he had stood at the piano with him for perhaps a decade, had the most dismal of stories that Tommy could imagine, which had only been elucidated to him one beer-soaked night in late

November. That lad had joined up as one of Kitchener's volunteers, proud and intent on serving his King and Country as so many started out as being. He suffered the monotony of the route marches and drills in and out of the rain on Salisbury Plain. He listened attentively to every lecture he was given, whether it was on firing his rifle, administering emergency first aid or how best to avoid venereal disease. And once he had been sent to Folkestone, he waited impatiently for his opportunity to be a hero. There in Kent each day would drag interminably. Each announcement that a new batch was to be shipped abroad was greeted with excited anticipation, then repeated despondency as his name got missed from the list of the chosen ones.

Then finally it was his turn. No more the drudgery of playing at soldiers, opportunity and glory beckoned.

The night on the boat to France was, and would remain, the worst and longest of his life. Packed tightly on deck all the lads competed for any essence of the comfort of a seat. Shoulder to shoulder, back-to-back, front-to-front they claimed their own personal space. The darkness of the night drew the boat out of the harbour and into the gently undulating waters.

The storm struck less than an hour after leaving port and it didn't relent until France was in sight. Willed on by the wind and the rain, the sea battered and thrashed against the boat intent on dragging it and all its cargo to their doom.

The men huddled, held tight and spewed their last meals as one animal.

Landing was a reward, and the purpose of their task was revitalised. Marching through the streets with children cheering and waving brought the cause to life and washed at least temporarily the stench of vomit from his great coat. Glory was short-lived. Crowded into a railway cattle truck with only slightly more room than the boat, he was only thankful that dark and small spaces were not a great fear of his. The train crawled to the lines. He tried to sleep, like they all did. Like most he failed. The hours stretched beyond his imagining with the trundling only occasionally punctuated by a piss or grub stop.

He arrived behind the lines, the least prepared for battle that he could ever have imagined. Exhausted and stinking, the last thing he felt he could do now was to face the Boche. Fortunately, he didn't have to. The workings of the war machine were now oiled and well-practiced. Bath houses and laundries freshened the outer layers, a straw filled billet in a barn relaxed the body before the drills and the parades were instigated. He could have been in Folkestone, or Salisbury Plain. Drills. Drills. Drills.

Eventually his moment came. The fruition of all his training and patience. Months of dedication. His life's purpose. The trenches.

Nothing that he had read about or heard talk about prepared him for the sheer disappointment of walking into the trenches for the first time. It wasn't the brisk march through golden gates with rifles held high and a fanfare of trumpets that his mind had conjured up, but a slow trudge down a muddy footpath onto sloping narrow duckboards. The outside world disappeared slowly as he sunk beneath the surface into another world. A world not of trophies and bravado, but dank dugouts, dirt and rats.

On his second day he was ordered for latrine duty. This was something that there had not been a lecture for or a special training session. The sergeant gave him the instructions with the orders, and he was expected to work the rest out by himself. It wasn't difficult. By his third run he had a process. Then the Minenwerfer struck. A solitary, almost accidental projection that was innocuous in the calmness of the sector. It surprised everyone, not least of all the lad. It landed a few short feet from him propelling him hard onto the trench wall. The duckboards splintered beneath him then shot upwards as if to escape their confines. One shard sought the lad out, zeroed in on his hand and duly tore the thumb off. The lad had scored the most sought after of goals, a blighty one.

Within weeks he was home in England, his war done, his duty fulfilled.

Whether round the piano or in any company, he rarely spoke of his horrendous experiences at the Front Line. How could he ever hope to answer his grandson with any modicum of pride when he asked, 'Grandad, tell me about your war. Did you kill any Germans?'

What could he say?

'Well, it was like this my boy, I was shovelling shit for a bit, then a bomb exploded right by me and it took off my thumb, then I got sent back home.'

Not the greatest of stories. He rarely spoke of his war.

But what they all conveyed around the piano, every single one of them was the sheer pride that they held in themselves and in each other. The knowing pride that they had changed the world. They had been the ones to create the country that they all now lived in. A country of health care and pensions and money for the unemployed. It may have taken another war to seal the deal, but they had set the ball rolling and they knew it.

Every Saturday Tommy was reminded, as they all sang around that piano, how much he loved his country. How proud he was of it. How proud he was of being a part of the making of it.

He felt a momentary spasm of pain in his ankle, and it made him think how, particularly this week, he believed in the fabulous country that they had.

A couple of weeks previously he had slipped on some leaves, or maybe it was a raised paving stone that he tripped on, or perhaps he had just lost his footing, he did that sort of thing these days. Whatever it was, all he knew was that one moment he had been marching to the Post Office without a care in the world and the next he was on his arse with a small crowd milling around him and a throbbing down by his foot. There was chatter and concerned questions. Arguing as some tried to raise him, and others insisting he stay put. At some stage someone must have called for an ambulance for it soon arrived vociferously as Tommy ridiculed the sympathy of his Samaritans.

He was in the hospital for two days with his leg raised a few inches from the bed. There was nothing broken, it was just a bad sprain. Something that needed to be taken care of, especially at his age, but nothing of a huge amount of concern. The young nurses clucked and fussed around him to which he responded with gruffness to hide his enjoyment. Then, with all parties happy with his condition, he was permitted to leave and return home.

A few days later, after finishing his dinner and returning to the front room with a hot mug of tea to while away some time playing patience, he was disturbed by a loud knocking on his front door. He had just placed his mug down on the table, picked up his pipe and with his knees half-bent was in the process of seeking out the leather upholstery of his dining chair with his backside. It wasn't an opportune moment for visitors.

'Oh fu—' he muttered, automatically looking toward the window to see if he could be seen from anyone outside. Calculating that he was in fact invisible he continued to lower himself onto his seat and began to light the pipe.

The door was struck again. Louder and more insistently.

'Bugger,' he said, knowing that he couldn't escape from his unwanted visitor.

'I'm coming,' he shouted, and using his stick as leverage he got himself back to his feet. 'I'm coming,' he repeated and shuffled slowly into the hallway and to the front door.

Through the three small, frosted glass panels near the top of the door he could discern the straight angles of a hat that was turning first one way then the other as the wearer was plainly turning their head as they awaited his arrival.

He fumbled with the safety chain, released it, and with one hand on the latch and the other struggling to turn the door-knob as well as hold onto his stick he tried to open the door. It wasn't an easy operation and it made him wish that he had continued to play possum and ignored the visitor. But finally, he succeeded, and he eased the door gently open. For a moment his attention was focussed on calculating where he should step, how to hold his stick, and most importantly how he could avoid losing his balance. Then, content with all the decisions he had made, he raised his head.

She was a vision.

Slim, brunette with sparkling eyes and an intoxicating beauty spot over the left side of her lip. She wore a nurse's costume. A nurse's uniform, Tommy's mind corrected.

She smiled with every part of her face and Tommy was, for only the second time in his life, profoundly and totally smitten.

'Mr Atkins?' she questioned.

Tommy's mouth dropped open, and he wordlessly nodded his head in acknowledgement. He hoped intensely that he wasn't feeling a small dribble in the corner of his mouth.

'Mr Atkins,' she went on. 'My name is Nurse Clarke. I have just come to see how your ankle is doing.'

Now this, thought Tommy was the kind of country that they had built, a great country, a caring country, a country fit for all. It was the sort of country that would send a beautiful young creature like Nurse Clarke to check up on an old fuddy duddy like him. It was his country.

Every Saturday they are all like-minded. Stood and sat around the piano, they all feel the same pride in what has been achieved and their role in it. And they are excited. Excited for the future. For the children and their grand-children and their great grand-children. They know that they are not for this world much longer, but that doesn't matter, as long as sanity and common sense prevails, they have built a country that can truly be and remain Great. Their excitement is palpable in their voices and their eyes and the way they hold themselves.

The thrill isn't dissimilar to the emotions they felt all those years back when they had been so much younger.

Tommy could remember that feeling easily, he could touch, he would almost say that he could smell it. August 1914. The whole country was holding its breath to see what Germany would do. Surely it would do the sensible thing, the right and proper thing and turn back and leave lowly, little Belgium in peace. Surely Germany wouldn't risk the ire of the British Empire?

They had until midnight, German time, to do the right thing. Britain waited. The hands of Big Ben revolved as a multitude of eyes watched on. The chimes rang out and the signal was given that Britain was now at war.

Tommy read the news in the paper the following morning and every part of him couldn't help but feel a sudden elation. It was fantastic news. It would be, for him, a rebirth. He had served his time once for King and Country, now he was being handed the opportunity to do so again, and in doing so he could be young again, have real purpose again.

The army had been his escape after his mother had died. He had done all he could for her in her last week's battling the torment that was consumption. She had worked for as long as she could hide her condition from her employers, but eventually it became too obvious and she was released with an apology, the money that she was owed and an extra two pounds for her immediate future. Tommy never heard or saw his mother cry, but that day that she came home he saw a sadness weighing her down that she couldn't disguise. He was fourteen and bringing home a small, but valuable wage from selling and delivering newspapers. She never told him that she was dying, and he never told her that he knew. He never questioned her not working, their lives simply transitioned, quietly and effortlessly.

She died with his hand in hers and a cold flannel on her forehead. There was a fire roaring in the hearth and fresh flowers on the table.

Tommy mourned the loss of his mother for the rest of his life, but he blamed no one or nothing for her death. It was just what happened. For a while he remained in the house that had been his home, but it soon became evident that he could never sell enough newspapers to pay the rent and eat, and besides, without his mother it was no longer home, it was simply cold walls sheltering him from the weather. He packed a bag one morning, just as he would do on so many occasions in his life, and left. If the army wouldn't have him then he would try the navy, if they wouldn't have him, then he would just see what came round the corner, there would be something, he was young and strong and could read and write.

The army did have him, welcomed him in as a boy soldier and he was given, in a signing of his name a new family. He never regretted, not for a moment, becoming a servant to the crown. There were tough days, many of them, when physical demands were made of him that every ounce of his body questioned his ability to answer successfully. There was abuse, both physical and mental, especially in the early years, from those that always looked for easy victims. But Tommy was tough. He was physically strong, and his brain was quick and smart. Few tried to bully him more than once, none did it more than twice.

Shortly after he had met and married his beautiful Alice, he was sent to South Africa to put the Boers back in their place. They had stepped out of line and given the British a good thrashing, so now it was time for reinforcements to right the wrongs. It was the first time that he had been on board a ship and it made him thankful that the army had taken him in, that he hadn't needed to enlist in the navy. He suffered atrociously for two weeks and then from nowhere he found his sea legs and never again would he suffer on the seas.

South Africa was hot, humid and full of flies but also rich with sights that he had never believed he would ever see. Animals that he had only read about or seen caged in the London Zoological Gardens, flowers and plants of every hue and people of such a dark ebony colour that it looked as if they shone when the sun caught them.

The Boers were vicious and merciless, guerrilla-like in their tactics against the organised lines and orders of the British Army. They fought with an intensity and courage of those protecting their homes and families. It was at Kimberley that he first took a life. A moment that passed instantly to the next. One shot, one face, one hole. A painless death of a nobody. The second life he took was with the next but one bullet that he fired. The eyes were bearing down on him, screams of anger belching from the mouth, arms and legs flailing. He seemed like an inhuman monster. Tommy's whole body was shaking as he hurried to make the shot, his eyes were filled with sweat, and the dust kicked up by the men engaged with each other. He squeezed the trigger of his Lee Enfield and the shot rang out. The monster was barely twelve feet from Tommy when the bullet ripped into his stomach. He crumpled immediately onto the ground spewing blood from the hole that had been bored into him. Tommy would never forget the eyes of the monster. They were the eyes of a father, a middle-aged man who was probably a farmer by the look of his thick set features. Those eyes were filled with the despair of failure and a sadness of a future that he couldn't provide for his loved ones. The mouth gurgled up an oxygen rich froth of blood which the monster spat out onto the ground in front of him. The eyes never left Tommy's. Hatred and anger emanated from them as if perhaps that could win his battle. He coughed and spluttered some more, and his hands gripped tightly to his wound as if he was only struck by an attack of chronic indigestion. Tommy watched, transfixed by the demon who had become a man who had become a father. Fear swept over Tommy. Not a fear of death or danger but a fear of his mortal soul. The man sat and bled. Silently dying in front. Silently and slowly.

It seemed that Tommy watched him die for hours on end, though in reality it was just a few minutes. When death finally came it came silently, unobtrusively. The eyes remained on Tommy, one moment glistening with life, the next dulled.

Tommy fought the Boers because it was his sworn duty and his job. He didn't regret those that he killed, or those that he saw killed in battle. Each side were fighting for what they believed was right. But he took home with him from South Africa the face of the farmer, ingrained in his mind, not as a nightmare or a beast, but a clear message and acknowledgement that those he killed were just men, nothing more, nothing less. Years later he would forget for a while that enemies were only enemies because others told him so. For a while he would believe the propaganda of monsters being in the midst of battle.

He had become a father whilst he had been in South Africa, but it was a knowledge that escaped him until he returned home. The arms of Alice were as warm and welcoming as he had expected and dreamed. The face of his son though was something that he hadn't been prepared for. The eyes that sparkled back at him on that first meeting silently instructed him of the path that his life must now take. They told him of his future responsibilities and the meaning that his own life held. When he took his son into his arms for the first time, he felt the promise of a future.

Tommy remained at home with his family only a short few weeks before he was again given orders that would take him away. Curzon in India required military reinforcements and Tommy was amongst those whose destinies lay to the east.

Leaving Alice and his fragile son creased Tommy with pain. Duty had to be done, orders had to be followed, but the definition of his life had changed, and he vowed in parting that his place was with his young family, not on the far side of the globe.

For Tommy, being sent to India was like being sent to purgatory. The sea passage held few fears for him, though passing the Cape of Good Hope challenged even his accustomed stomach. But it was a long and arduous journey during which ennuie was the biggest malaise. India was filled with colours and scents like nothing he had seen in Africa. It was heart-stoppingly beautiful, rich in so many ways.

Curzon sent them to Tibet on a mission that Tommy never understood. They had been told they were to defend against the

Russians but the only ones they fought and killed were poorly armed and ill trained villagers. The whole experience left Tommy feeling empty. The duty to King and Country had been surpassed by a duty to his family, the cause for which he was prepared to lay down his very life was now no longer the one that paid him, but one which yearned for his comfort and presence. When he sailed from India it was to return and embrace his life as a father.

His son's childhood consumed Tommy. They were blissful years filled with meaning and love. Where once he needed the army to fill a void, now he required nothing but the love of his wife and the arms of his son. Nothing else mattered. But the years stretched on and although love never diminished between any of them, the completeness of caring for a vulnerable child inevitably dwindles as they become self-sufficient and able to look after themselves.

Increasingly Tommy felt less than what he had been. Each day that he opened up the grocery shop that he had run since leaving the army, he felt that a little part of him was dying. That he was being slowly eroded. Alice would always have his heart, but his reason for being was questioned when his child no longer needed him as much as he had done. As the natural love and pride that a son has for his father flickers, dims and often disappears as the son sees only a man, not a hero, so Tommy felt the loss. And questioned his own existence.

The monotony of his work-days were no longer a gift so that he could spend time with his family but a curse highlighting his own deficiencies. Hour after hour he would see himself filling sacks with carrots, turnips, cabbages, potatoes, swedes. It became a life that he couldn't be proud of. An existence that he couldn't abide. He craved for his youth. He craved to be somebody again. Just one last time.

That was what August 4, 1914 gave him, what war offered, the chance to have a purpose again. Alice saw the change come over him immediately. Before her eyes he became younger, his shoulders went back, and his head seemed to raise. He looked up from the newspaper and she saw in his eyes a light that had been lost for so long.

'You want to go don't you,' she stated.

'My love, I have to go,' he replied, he could scarcely conceal his excitement. 'It's my duty.'

'No Tom,' she responded. 'Duty has nothing to do with it. You have done your duty for this country and if not for this particular king, definitely for the crown. This is for you and you know it is.'

Tommy looked deeply into her eyes. There wasn't anger lying there, but there was a sadness and a shimmer of fear, but overall, there was an acceptance.

'It is for me Alice, I need this. I have been dying and I want to live again, just one more time. This will all be blown over in a few months, Christmas at the outside, I just want to be part of something again, just for a moment.'

'It's fine Tom, I'll be fine, we'll be fine. Go and do your bit, then come back and get old with me.'

There was the evident sound of fast running feet outside and suddenly the back door burst open.

'Have you seen the news? It's happened. We're going to war,' their son was an explosion of excited information.

'We've heard,' Alice responded blankly.

The boy's beaming face dropped slightly at the tone of his mother's voice and with some puzzlement he looked from his mother, to his father and then back to his mother. He saw something in her eyes and then with realisation turned back to his father.

'You're going to go aren't you Dad? You're going to go and kick those German backsides out of Belgium.'

'I, I don't know,' Tommy stuttered, looking at Alice as much in apology as for confirmation.

'Yes, you are, I know you are. You'll show them Dad, they'll soon start running when the great Tommy Atkins gets over there.' The boy chattered excitedly as he ran to his father and threw his arms about his neck, hugging him passionately.

Tommy felt a surge of self-pride and worth flood into his body like an electric shock. He grabbed his boy who was now almost the same height as he was and gave him a bear hug.

'You're right. I am going, but it won't be for long, just until Christmas or thereabouts they say, then we'll have them on the run.'

For a moment Alice looked at her two boys, years apart in age but so close in mentality. Then she turned to the kitchen sink, picked up a cloth and began to dry off the dishes that were lying there. One solitary tear left her eye and dribbled half-way down her cheek before she wiped it away with the cloth.

Tommy sorted his affairs out that day. It wasn't a hard task, there was a fervour gripping everyone and Tommy announcing to his boss that he wanted to re-enlist met with heartfelt approval. They agreed that he would work for the rest of the week and that Tommy's son would be taken on as an interim measure until the new year.

The week then dragged for Tommy but sped by for Alice who seemed to be the only one not able to greet the conflict with a sense of excitement. Then on Saturday morning he went down to the Church Hall where they were attesting. The queue of men that wound from the hall stretched fifty yards even at the early hour that Tommy joined it. Moments after he had joined the line it expanded to twice the length. It was a line of the greatest cross-section imaginable. Tommy could easily pick out the ones like himself, the old sweats who had already worn the khaki and served their time. It wasn't just their age, but their bearing that couldn't be disguised and in their faces their experiences were moulded. He saw in them the anticipation that he felt, the gift of a return to their youth.

Others in the line were not much more than boys, not even much older than his own son. Their faces were clean and innocent, to them they were being offered not their youth, but their manhood and they were grasping out for it eagerly. Some were scrawny with moth-eaten rags for clothes. Dirt clung to their complexions and their eyes were nervous and desperate. No doubt, Tommy concluded, these saw the war as an opportunity for a hot meal, a roof above their heads, employment.

Then there were those that bore themselves with confidence. They wore suits that depicted, if not wealth, at least a comfortable income. Their skin didn't sag off their faces and bones but was smoothed by the fullness of flesh. Some of these looked down on those around them, some of them smiled welcomingly to all. What did they seek in the war Tommy wondered? It wasn't a hot meal, or even their youth, for most of these were mature but still young. Maybe it was the taste of adventure. Maybe it was an escape from whatever monotony that their lives held. Quite possibly they just wanted to see foreign lands.

And then there were those who were furtive. They stood in line nervously, constantly counting the numbers in front of them, checking the lines both in front and behind, searching for someone or something. Watching out for their own discovery. These were men that acted like rats chased into the sewer. Maybe this was for them the line out of the sewer. A route to a new life, different opportunities. To Tommy they stunk of criminality, doubtless they were known to the law, the war to them was an escape.

There were others that were shifty and nervous, that queued impatiently and held their heads down, their eyes covered, hats concealing much of their faces to a casual passer-by. Who were they escaping? Tommy questioned himself. They appeared and acted guiltily, but it wasn't a criminal guilt, it was more of a personal guilt. They were in hiding, they were trying to deceive someone, somewhere. Their wives perhaps? Girlfriends? Cuckolded husbands?

Tommy observed them all with an interest. The queue moved slowly so he had time to observe and conclude. There were many who were lined up with friends, some with family members. They talked loudly and vigorously together, buoyed by being able to share in the experience. But Tommy held his own counsel. He stood patiently, smoked his pipe casually and watched with interest. The more that he watched, the more that he felt at home and the more that he felt his actions were just and right.

Slowly that church door consumed the line of men, swallowed them up inside. One by one they entered willingly, stepped in voluntarily and with smiles on their faces.

There were none in that queue that day that Tommy ever recalled seeing afterwards. After he was beckoned forward, answered some basic questions and signed his name he was momentarily regurgitated back into his life, just as they all were. It would be on another day that they would be called to fulfil their obligation. And that day came soon. Tommy would wonder how many of them failed in their quest to become soldiers, how many were turned away, how many of them cursed with disappointment at their failure. How many, he also wondered, subsequently cursed at the success of their acceptance.

Which ones joined him in service to king and country from that long queue he never knew, but he did know that many would have done and countless others in similar lines the length and breadth of the country and the Empire. And that with their signatures duly signed they made the passage over the waters.

It was a regular thought to Tommy and had been since returning to Flanders alone, after Alice, of all those that went across. How many had gone? Hundreds of thousands doubtlessly, perhaps millions even. So many. And he knew that most of them had come back, not all perhaps in the same condition as when they went over, but most of them did come back, of that there was no question. But too many, far too many still remained over there in France, in Flanders, on the Western Front. Some of them had stones that told the reader where they lay, others rested anonymously. He thought about them often in his everyday life, they would greet him in his mind, jumping in there at random times, usually they still surprised by their appearance. He was however never surprised by them on a Saturday night. At the club, as the keys of the piano were pounded and voices were joined together, he conjured them up consciously and always held them in his thoughts. None of them were forgotten to Tommy.

Tommy still needed the walking stick when he joined the trip that the Legion arranged that year. He went every year without fail on the trips. They were simple affairs run by the Legion for any of the old boys like him or any club members that wanted to go over and pay their respects to their husbands or fathers or grandfathers. A small fleet of coaches would take them to Dover and then over to Dunkerque, and from there they would be taken to whichever region had been decided upon. Simple hotels or even sometimes guest houses were booked in Ypres itself or Arras, Albert, Poperinge, Mons. Nothing fancy, but always comfortable. The old boys that joined the trips always had their costs subsidised by the club, it was for them as much for the ones that they went to see, that the trips were arranged.

It didn't matter where they were headed, Tommy would never consider not going. He felt that he had trodden on every inch of soil that had been tainted by that war, so it didn't matter where he returned to. It held no ghosts for him to exorcise, but there was an obligation for him to return, always, for as long as he was able. So that they knew that he had not forgotten.

It was to the Ypres Salient that they were returning that year, and they had rooms booked in a half dozen establishments in Poperinge. Tommy, along with seven others had a bed arranged at the old Talbot House, which still stood proudly and still welcomed in pilgrims to the town. Tommy hadn't been back inside the place since he had read in its garden and played on its billiards table back before Third Ypres. After the war it had been returned by the army to its owner, so even when Tommy was at Tyne Cot, he didn't feel inclined to go and revisit the place, even out of curiosity, but then, in the interim years, it had once again become a hostel. As the great front door was pushed and held open for him to enter, Tommy could feel the presence of his past. The hallway expanded in front of him, and he stepped slowly in, aided by his stick and joined by his fellow tourists. Apart from them, and the wardens that welcomed them all, the hall and seemingly the house, was empty. Warm and welcoming, but empty.

The first time that Tommy had entered Talbot House it was far from being empty, it had been as full as any house could possibly be. The hall had been crowded with men chatting loudly together, drinking from mugs or chomping on biscuits. There was movement everywhere, from the kitchen to the hall, from the hall to the upstairs, from a side room to the hall, or back the other way. There were those leaving the hallway to go outside to the garden passing others coming into the warmth. Somewhere a piano played with voices belching out the words, elsewhere, dimly and far above him he could make out the more sentient chords of an organ and the serious tones of men praising their god in song. It was a house brimming with life at a time when death and the sight of it was a far too familiar and accepted part of the norm.

Stepping into Talbot House was an escape for Tommy, as indeed for all who entered, from the sights, sounds and odours of the war that surrounded him and he would subsequently become a frequent visitor. Sometimes he would stay just a few minutes to fleetingly reacquaint himself with the atmosphere, other times he would stay for hours. It was always a noisy house, that was inevitable through the sheer numbers of inhabitants, and when his mood was right it was the noise that he craved, the noise that was a semblance of normality. Other times he sought the quieter parts of the house, he would exchange his cap in temporary loan for a book from the cupboard that professed to be a library and take it to the far end of the garden seeking out a small space that could be his, for a while. In those moments of reading, he could be transported to his son's night-time bed of perhaps a decade before, or even to a corner of his own childhood, a chair by a glowing fire after a warm bath and his mother baking bread.

Occasionally, Tommy would even venture high into the house, to the tiny chapel in the attic where the custodian, Reverend Philip (Tubby to those who knew him) Clayton, might be taking a service. Tubby had become a huge name to all the lads that walked through any part of the Ypres Salient and Tommy would see him often in the house and even sometimes in the lines when he would pitch up seemingly from nowhere with a battered little organ that appeared to buckle at its sides. The small clergyman would pound away at the keys of that organ vainly trying to overpower the din of the shells, but nevertheless, through sheer enthusiasm and energy, pulling the spirits of the lads along with him. Tubby's was a familiar face to Tommy, but he never attempted to make his own face a familiar one to Tubby. Something in the lack of his own religious convictions prevented him from stepping over the boundary of familiarity, somehow, he didn't ever feel worthy. He had known then that it was his own insecurities that were at fault, the reverend had always insisted that the House and all who entered it were to be treated evenly, religious affiliations or rank bore no effect or held no privilege. Yet, deep inside Tommy always felt too ordinary. Now as he walked into the hallway once again, he felt and knew that it was his ordinariness that this house had always been designed for.

There was much that Tommy remembered, artefacts that had been recaptured or replaced. Some of the old signs that Tubby had written to try and keep order in the house without having to stipulate any rules and regulations. Silly signs that played on a man's conscience and encouraged him to behave, "If you are in the habit of spitting on the carpet at home, please spit here", "never judge a man by his umbrella, it may not be his", "the wastepaper baskets are purely ornamental". Wandering around the rooms on the ground floor, there was much that was familiar, not necessarily the furniture itself, but the placings that it took in the rooms and although in these moments they lay empty, Tommy could see the chairs filled with countless anonymous faces that were all different and yet all, absolutely the same.

The guests were shown to their simple quarters upstairs, they were the same basic rooms that had been offered, for a fee, to officers during the war in order to help fund the running of the house. Tommy was to share his room with two others. He sat down on the bunk and once again he felt returned to another time. Perhaps it was during the great conflict, a bunk in barracks before they had come over the channel, or perhaps it was another bunk when he had been much younger, hardly more than a boy, who knew little of soldiering, or then again maybe it was a bunk from not such a long time ago, a bed in a room when he had first returned to Belgium in a small guest house that would become his home for so many months.

As he was joined in the room, he saw them as the world saw them, three old men, crippled with age, slow in their motions, their eyes and ears fogged from their experiences of life. To the world they had little left to offer, just a cost, an encumbrance to society. Then he saw them as they saw themselves, no older or younger than they had ever been, three lads sharing a room together. One of them loudly and grotesquely farted and they all burst out laughing.

'I didn't need my hearing aid on for that you filthy old bastard,' Tommy said.

'I hope that was just a fart, if that had been me my trousers would be spilling shit now,' the other chimed in.

A coach had been arranged to take the whole group into Ypres that evening for a collective meal at The Trumpet, a decent restaurant in the square that served fries as a side to every order. When it pulled up into the square Tommy felt as he always did in returning to the Belgian town, that he was once again home. There was a comfort, understanding and welcome in Ypres that had never been dissolved by the passing of years. Tommy passed up the meal and took himself off on his own. His small stick clicking regularly on the cobblestoned streets he wandered down the familiar roads that had hardly changed for thirty years. There were few people meandering around and those that he did pass were clearly locals. At the Menin Gate he took a right then a small upward path on to the ramparts. He didn't walk far from the gate, though in his mind he took all the steps to the garden he had encountered back when he had first returned after the war. He found himself a bench and set himself down. There was a gentle breeze, but it wasn't cold. He sat and emptied his mind. Home. It was, in so many ways, his home, their home. He had bypassed Ypres when he first landed in France and was sent directly to Fromelles, but those that had come across earlier all spoke of the town and how it was the heart of the conflict. It had become a town of mythical stature, it must be defended at all cost, if they were ever to lose Ypres then they would surely lose the war, the Germans would make a straight line to the Belgian ports and the game would be over. Now he could remember marching through the Lille Gate the first time and feeling the shock of the already great destruction that it had suffered. It was a battered and bruised town, but it was full of life, khaki swarmed all over it, engulfing every crack and crevice.

Tommy would get to know Ypres intimately in those years and despite it always being the gateway to hell, it was also the gateway out of hell. It became the home that you were desperate not to leave and the one you hankered to return to.

He sat, quietly and contentedly. Then, when it felt about right, he pulled himself once more to his feet and walked to the steps of the Menin Gate and stepped slowly down, back to the level of the street. He was exactly in the middle of the gates amongst a small gathering of people, mainly they were those from the Legion who had come across with him to Belgium that morning. There weren't many and they were dwarfed by the scale of the gate and the seemingly infinite number of names engraved all over it.

Presently two buglers dressed in the black overcoats of the Ypres Fire Service shuffled up past Tommy and made their way towards the far end where they waited patiently, chatting quietly to each other and occasionally checking their watches. When they agreed that the time was right they marched formally and respectfully to the middle of the road, presented their bugles to their lips and simultaneously projected those haunting first notes of The Last Post.

Heads were bowed all around him and apart from the bugles there was only the quiet sound of breathing. Tommy however held his head high, watching the two men, listening intently to every note. Still, after all these years, the lost were being honoured by Belgium and pride swelled his heart. They hadn't been forgotten and he hadn't been forgotten, they were all remembered for what they had done and what they had given for Belgium's liberation.

The buglers finished their tribute and lowered their instruments. A man stepped forward from the pavement into the centre of the road and began to speak the familiar words of Binyon from the second stanza of his poem, The Fallen. Then as he finished a gentle murmur echoed his words.
'We Will Remember Them.'

They made an early start the next morning with the coach picking them up in the Poperinge town square at half past eight. There was a schedule that had been advertised and explained, but these trips were as much about fulfilling individual requests to visit loved ones as it was taking in the sights and memorials. It was always the lost that were given priority. And so, Tommy took his place in the coach and waited to see where they would end up.

At each stop he would descend from the vehicle and then step away from the other members of his group. It was the way he acted every year. Whether it was a memorial that they were shown like that at Vancouver Corner, or a still present bunker like that on Hill 60, or a garden of those that had been lost, he would lose himself in his own thoughts and recollections. In each garden he would wander down the lines taking in the names, the ages, the regiments and always seek out the soldier that was known only unto God. There he would stop, kneel down slowly and touch the ground tenderly, before returning to the waiting coach.

Shortly before midday they pulled into a small tree-lined lane that was muddy and barely gravelled. The coach driver was muttering something under his breath that was clearly a disgruntlement at being asked to take this godforsaken road. He finally pulled alongside the tall white archway that denoted the entrance to Sanctuary Wood Cemetery, the headstones lay stretched in largely uniform order before them, with no wall separating them from the road. This had been Tommy's choice, it was a whim really, feeling perhaps that by staying at Talbot House he ought to pay his respects to Gilbert who lay there and whose name had been given to the house in Poperinge.

They all sifted out and Tommy stepped away. In his one hand his stick gave him support, in his other he held a small bag. He knew roughly where Gilbert lay as he had been there before to seek him out, many years before and then just out of curiosity. He headed through the arch and into the garden, for that was what it would always be to Tommy. Then he walked steadily, perusing and reflecting on a headstone here, another one there, moving gently through. He had to search for a while for Gilbert as his memory wasn't perfect, but then he found it, towards the back on the left, facing the wrong way. He found it, read the name and quietly touched its top.

'God bless you Gilbert,' he spoke gently, automatically paying homage to the god that had been such a large part of the young man's life.

Then Tommy looked up and around as if surveying the scene. He stepped away from Gilbert and walked along the lines behind the Sword of Sacrifice. He sought out, as he did in each garden, one that was only known to God.

Many here were fortunate, they had not died and been lost anonymously, they had been buried by those who knew them, maybe not known them in life, but who knew their names when they had passed.

Then Tommy came to him. He was there as he always was. Known unto God. But Tommy knew him as well as he always knew him.

He was at the end of a row, so Tommy eased himself down beside him, struggling awkwardly so that he could sit with his legs stretched out in front. He opened up his bag and took out an apple, a small flask and the sandwich that he had made that morning in the kitchen at Talbot House. Then he began to speak, quietly but not whispering.

'It's been a good year mate, your cousins are good girls and they come and keep an eye on me', he took a bite of his apple, glancing round casually, then continued between chewing. 'Did myself a mischief the other week, what a clumsy fucker I am, went down like a sack of spuds in the street, twisted my ankle something rotten and spent a couple of nights in the hospital, but you know what, this beautiful nurse, she came round to see me after I was home, just to check up on me and the ankle. What a looker she was. She even stayed for a cuppa and a slice of Cousin Dolly's fruit cake. What a treat. What a lucky fella I am, I mean no disrespect to your mother or nothing, but it was a fine tasting cake.'

Tommy opened up his flask and poured some tea into the beaker. Steam drifted up from it and he blew it gently away before testing the liquid with his lips.

'You know it's all down to you son, you know that don't you? These wonderful nurses that come out and look after us all. You did that. You've given us a wonderful country my boy, a country to be proud of. You should be proud. I'm proud. Proud of you. So very much.'

Tommy stalled; emotion pinched him as it always had done.

'I miss you my boy, miss you so much you will never know. I miss you every single day. There is nothing that I wouldn't do if I could have had you with me. All these hospitals and free doctors and money for us old uns and everything, I would have swapped in an instant to have you with me all these years, but of course, I know I could never have that. So, I'll just miss you and I'll love you for always. But I will never stop missing you and I'll never stop loving you and I will never ever forget what you did for us, all of us.'

A tear rolled down his cheek and he let it, he always did, it was his gift to himself to let his feelings out once a year at the side of his son. He finished his sandwich quietly, whilst his right hand rested on the top of the stone as if round the shoulders of his boy. For a while no words needed to be shared.

Then the sound of the coach's engine starting up brought

Tommy round.

'I've got to go now my boy. I love you. I'll always love you.'

He took up his walking stick and pressed it hard into the ground, then placing all his weight on it he pushed. For a moment he was almost standing, the sun was bright and there were birds singing in the nearby trees. Then he felt a sudden, brief punch in his heart and the world swam around him. His legs gave way, and he began to stumble. He dropped the stick and grasped for the stone as his legs melted beneath him. With a jolt his backside struck the ground, and he was once again sat upright with his arm resting on the top of the stone. For a moment he gulped for breath. Then his mind eased, panic was erased and an all-encompassing calm washed over him.

THE END